Celestial Lights

Also by Cecile Pin
Wandering Souls

Celestial Lights
Cecile Pin

4th ESTATE • *London*

4th Estate
An imprint of HarperCollins*Publishers*
1 London Bridge Street
London SE1 9GF

www.4thestate.co.uk

HarperCollins*Publishers*
Macken House
39/40 Mayor Street Upper
Dublin 1
D01 C9W8
Ireland

First published in Great Britain in 2026 by 4th Estate

1

Copyright © Cecile Pin 2026

Cecile Pin asserts the moral right to be identified as the author of this work in accordance with the Copyright, Designs and Patents Act 1988

A catalogue record for this book is available from the British Library

ISBN 978-0-00-870639-5 (hardback)
ISBN 978-0-00-870640-1 (trade paperback)

This novel is entirely a work of fiction. The names, characters and incidents portrayed in it are the work of the author's imagination. Any resemblance to actual persons, living or dead, events or localities is entirely coincidental.

All rights reserved. No part of this publication may be reproduced, stored in a retrieval system, or transmitted, in any form or by any means, electronic, mechanical, photocopying, recording or otherwise, without the prior permission of the publishers.

Without limiting the exclusive rights of any author, contributor or the publisher of this publication, any unauthorised use of this publication to train generative artificial intelligence (AI) technologies is expressly prohibited. HarperCollins also exercise their rights under Article 4(3) of the Digital Single Market Directive 2019/790 and expressly reserve this publication from the text and data mining exception.

Set in Adobe Garamond Pro by Six Red Marbles UK, Thetford, Norfolk

Printed and bound in the UK [using 100%
renewable electricity at CPI Group (UK) Ltd]

'There was a time when meadow, grove, and stream,
The Earth, and every common sight,
    To me did seem
    Apparelled in celestial light'

William Wordsworth, 'Ode: Intimations of Immortality from Recollections of Early Childhood'

'I cannot find a word to say to him; I cannot ask him anything at all; I cannot even look him in the face.'

Homer, *The Odyssey*, translated by E. V. Rieu

PART I

1

I was born the day *Challenger* fell out of the sky, and I was born blue. At least, that is what I was told.

My mother went into the maternity ward around the time the crew made its way to the shuttle – a giant, blood-orange tank from which hung the orbiter and the rocket boosters. If you watch videos from that day, you can see the crew as they leave their base, wide smiles and eighties hair, their sky-blue NASA uniforms visible from afar. It was an unusually chilly morning in Florida, but even so, hundreds of people came to Cape Canaveral to send them off. They had caps and T-shirts and cheering banners, cameras and binoculars at the ready.

Space launches did not usually attract so much attention, but *Challenger* was no ordinary launch. It held a teacher on board, Christa McAuliffe, who would be the first civilian in space. Just before she enters the shuttle, a ground-team member gives her an apple, bright red. As she says her thanks, cheerful, she turns the fruit over in her hands, admiring it closely, as though it were a planet itself, as though it held a whole world she had yet to explore.

Seventy-three seconds after lift-off, a heavy cloud of smoke and flames engulfed *Challenger*. It began breaking apart, its wreckage tumbling into the Atlantic Ocean. The crowd watched the fragments plummet, the billowing fumes they left in their wake, as confusion gave way to realisation and dread. There were no survivors on board. Later that day, President Reagan addressed his nation, quoting the poet John Gillespie Magee Jr., 'We will never forget them, nor the last time we saw them, this morning, as they prepared for their journey and waved goodbye and *slipped the surly bonds of earth to touch the face of God.*'

Later on, the investigation revealed that the failure at launch had been due to the temperature, much lower than expected. The small rubber O-rings, which were supposed to seal the joints of the rocket's segments, were stiffened by the cold and rendered brittle, causing fatal gas leaks. NASA had been advised by their engineers to postpone the launch, but too much was riding on it. Television crews and students watching from all over the country, all holding their breath, their childhood dreams, all holding some intangible hope on this launch. NASA decided to go ahead.

The names of the seven astronauts were: Christa McAuliffe, Francis R. Scobee, Michael J. Smith, Ronald E. McNair, Ellison S. Onizuka, Judith A. Resnik and Gregory B. Jarvis. If you watch videos from that day, you'll see them smiling as they leave their base, yes, and you'll see McAuliffe being handed the apple. And before that you'll see them having breakfast together, white-frosted cake emblazoned with the mission's logo. They're chatting and posing for the cameras, not a worry in sight – like they're going on a trip to the shop down the road, nothing extraordinary, nothing surreal, nothing that would take them out of this world and into the pitch-black skies.

It was around lift-off, across the Atlantic Ocean in a hospital near the village I would grow up in, that my mother gave a final push. I was quiet when the doctor first held me, and underneath the blood and slime my skin had a pale, ice-blue hue. My father assumed the worst. Not one to parade his emotions, he left the room dazed and numb, crouched in the corridor, and held his head in his hands. But as he was about to cry for the loss of his son, he heard tiny wails coming from the ward. He got up and ran back in, where he saw a nurse gently place me in my mother's arms, the blue already fading from my face. My cries grew louder as my breathing deepened and then, like the rarest of miracles and the most common of occurrences, there was life.

It's funny. In my head, these events are perfectly clear – their hidden corners, their pervading emotions, heightened and tangible. But when I try to recall my actual memories, I see that they're much more slippery.

Lately, I've been thinking of the summer of '95. The simmering heat, my feet cool against the kitchen tiles, the hovering flies and the sound of the milk as I poured it into my glass in the morning. But when I try to picture these moments, I can only do so for an instant. I see them as flashing images, as if looking through a View-Master at glimpses of my childhood. And all I'm left with are its lingering qualities, like an aftertaste that is bitter and sweet. Sometimes, I wonder if childhood is best described as a feeling, rather than a period of one's life. But what I do remember vividly, from that summer in the village when I was nine, is meeting Philly.

I'd just finished helping my father in the garage. He liked renovating old cars and selling them on, and that summer, it was a sixties Mini. 'Ollie,' Mum said, as I entered our house. She'd been in the garden and her cheeks were flushed. She removed a strand of blonde hair that had stuck to her forehead, her movements sluggish in the heat. 'Do you mind dropping off some of our plums to Mrs Tan?'

'Sure,' I said.

'Thank you, darling. Make sure you're back before sunset, okay? You know how your father gets if you're late.'

I nodded, took the plums and my bike, and I was off.

Mrs Tan lived on the other side of the village, past the old church and the Shield and Joe Harding's field, which stank of manure most of the year. The smell would invade Mrs Tan's house, and to cover it she sprayed perfume on her velvet cushions. I never asked her what it was, but sometimes a whiff of it will hit me as I'm walking down the street, or when I'm at a party, or in a lift – a light, woody, citrus smell – and I'm brought back to Mrs Tan's house.

But that day, instead of Mrs Tan, a girl about my age opened the door. She wore a pale-yellow dress that was smudged with grass, and her knees were covered with dirt. Her hair was tied into a dishevelled plait that came down to her waist, and her eyes were a colour I'd never seen before – a mix of brown and green and gold. She was pretty, I thought.

'Is Mrs Tan here?' I asked.

'Auntie Mel?' she said. 'She's gone to play cards at her friend's house. Why do you want to see her?'

I showed her my basket of plums. 'From our garden. My mum wanted me to bring them to her.'

She grabbed one and, before I had time to protest, took

a bite out of it. Juice splashed on her chin and dribbled onto her dress. 'You're lucky,' she said, her mouth half-full. 'Auntie Mel doesn't have fruit trees. I'm Philly, by the way.' She reached out her sticky hand for me to shake. I had oil stains on mine, which I hoped she wouldn't notice.

'I'm Oliver. But you can call me Ollie.'

'Okay. I will.'

'Philly's a nickname too, isn't it?'

'Yes.' She paused for a moment. 'But I won't tell you my full name, if that's what you're asking. I don't like it.'

'But I've told you mine,' I said. 'Is it Phyllis? Philippa?'

She shook her head and I stood there, basket in hand, uncomfortable.

'Do you really want to know?' she asked.

'It's not that. I just think it's fair that we know each other's name.'

She considered this. 'I'll tell you what. If you help me in the garden, I'll tell you.'

'Help you with what?'

'Come,' she said. 'You'll see.' She went past me and out of the house, rushing to the gate at the side. I followed suit in a stiff, slow run, not wanting the plums to spill everywhere.

When I think of the garden now, I picture freshly cut grass and roses everywhere, flawless and fragrant and towering over us. I see it as endlessly vast, but in truth, it couldn't have been much larger than a tennis court. It was on a slope and gave way to the river, which divided the village in two. 'This way!' Philly said. She hurried down to the bottom of the garden, her plait bouncing on her back as she ran.

By the time I'd caught up she was crouched under the old sycamore. She held a magnifying glass in her hand, its wooden handle scratched and faded. I observed her as she went from one patch of grass to the next, peering at it with great focus. The tree shaded us from the sun, and a warm breeze brushed against the lawn and Philly's dress. I crouched next to her. 'What are we looking for?' I asked.

'Shhh.' She put her index finger on my mouth. I felt my whole face blushing. 'Can you hear it?'

I listened closely. I could hear the wind cradling the sycamore, the river's flow and bees circling the roses. I could hear cars and Joe's tractor in the distance, but whatever Philly was referring to was lost on me.

'Hear what?'

'That very high-pitched buzz. Listen.'

We fell quiet again, and I pricked up my ears. And then, underneath the wind and the river, the bees and the cars and Joe's tractor, I heard a hum, barely discernible, but undoubtedly there. I nodded, and Philly smiled.

'*Cicadetta montana*,' she said. 'New Forest cicada.'

In response to my confused face she added, as if it was the most obvious of things, 'The insect!'

She seized a book that lay behind her and placed it on her lap, leafing through the pages.

'There.' She pointed at a photograph of a large, winged insect, its body black and orange. 'Most cicadas are very loud, sometimes as loud as motorcycles,' she said. 'But not the New Forest. This one is so high-pitched, adults can't hear it.' I smiled back at her. 'It's the only cicada species you can find here,' she went on, 'in the UK. They spend almost ten years growing underground, and when they're ready they come up to the surface for one last spring, lay their eggs, and after that they die.' She studied the page. 'Isn't that sad? They only get to be outside for a few weeks. Auntie Mel says I'm crazy to spend my whole day here searching for them. But she can't hear them. She doesn't understand.'

She looked up at me, as if for approval. Truthfully, I didn't have much sympathy: I've never been one for insects. I was tempted to say something mean-spirited, like I imagined the boys in my class would have done, that her aunt was right or that I really couldn't care less about any of this. But I took her in again. The magnifying glass was too big in her hands, and her dress was tight on her, as if she had outgrown it a summer ago.

'Well, let's search for them together, then,' I said. 'I'll

have a look on that side, and you here. You keep the magnifier. I have good eyes.'

We stood up. Philly patted her dress, removing the dirt and grass that clung to it.

'And then,' I added, 'you'll tell me your name?'

'Okay. Deal.'

We spent the whole afternoon looking for the cicadas, taking on our own patches of grass and eating plums, staying cool under the swaying shadows of the sycamore. We didn't say much to one another, yet an ease settled between us as the day went on. Philly's plait brushed against the earth as she examined it. I didn't care much about cicadas, no, but by the time I noticed the sun begin to slip behind the tree, I knew I wanted to spend the whole summer searching for them.

I got up so suddenly I startled Philly. 'Sorry,' I told her. 'I've gotta go.'

'But we haven't found them yet.'

I hesitated. 'I'm sorry. I have to be home before it gets dark. But maybe . . . maybe we can try again, if you'd like.'

Without meeting her eyes, I ran up the slope. Before opening the gate, I glanced back at the garden one last time. Philly stood there, magnifying glass in one hand, book in the other, looking at me. I saw that I'd forgotten the basket, now empty of plums. I made a start to go back for it, but then I feared that if I did, nightfall would catch up with me. After a brief wavering, I left it there on the lawn, toppled on the grass next to her. I turned away from the garden, and as I shut the gate, a wave of shame swept over me.

When I arrived home, shortly after sunset, my father sent me up to my room without dinner. To pass the time I started playing with my superhero figurines. Downstairs, my mother spoke in strained whispers. I opened my door by a shred. 'He was only half an hour late,' I heard her say. 'There was no need for that, Lar.' I closed my door quietly and went back to my figurines, making up an elaborate plot in which Superman and Gambit had to save Earth from an incoming meteor strike. Superman and Gambit were my favourites. They weren't like other superheroes, rich or bitten by radioactive spiders, or experimented on. Rather, they were *born* extraordinary. It wasn't an alter ego they had to conceal to fit in but their true selves. I liked that idea a lot: that someone's oddness could be their exceptionality. 'You're too tough on him,' Mum said downstairs, her voice raised just enough to pierce the floor beneath me. 'He's only a boy.'

I was starving and restless, and I was woeful. Not so much because I'd been grounded, but because the more I replayed the afternoon in my head, the more I was convinced that I'd made a fool of myself. I'd run away too quickly, cowardly, and I'd not found a single cicada. I hadn't even got Philly's full name. I put aside my superhero figurines, as if I was undeserving of them, and nose-dived into my bed.

Once the strained whispers had stopped, replaced by the low sound of the nine o'clock news, I heard my mother coming up the stairs. It was easy to recognise my parents' footsteps. Hers were quicker, lighter, less ominous than my father's. She gave my door a delicate knock. 'Ollie?' she said. I lay stiff on the bed. There was the clink of cutlery, and something being left on the floor, Mum's footsteps receding. The smell of grilled meat slowly reached me. I got up and opened the door, and there, on the landing, was a tray with a plate of potatoes, green beans and two sausages. I brought it to my room, and when I put the plate on my knees, sitting on the edge of my bed, it was still warm.

I woke up the next morning feeling blue. As on most early mornings my parents were asleep, so I went down the stairs as quietly as I could. The village slowly rose around me, the postman beginning his route. As I passed the front door on my way to the kitchen, I caught, out of the corner of my eye, a piece of torn paper that someone had slipped through the door. I have it with me, up here on *Talos*. It's tucked neatly into my journal, and when I long for home I'll reach for it, careful not to tear its edges, careful not to let it float away – a tangible proof that Earth was once my home and my entire world, that my memories, as slippery as they are, don't fool me completely. That there was a day, back in the summer of '95, when I picked up this note from the mat, and broke into a smile. For it said, in scrawly yet poised writing: *It's Philomena.*

PHOENIX MISSION
Commander Oliver Ines's Personal Log

Talos, Day 402. We're getting near to Mars's orbit: thermal control is working as planned, but the heat is making us lethargic.

Earth is now a pale blue smudge. Morale is good so far, but I worry what'll happen when it's no longer visible. We've had no contact with Earth for almost a year now, so having it within our sights feels like our only anchor. I often catch Shane and Lucia looking out through the round window, as if willing it to stay, to accompany us on our ten-year journey.

We've been trained for this, of course. We've been tested and observed. But I think, deep down, we know that nothing can prepare us for that juncture. Nothing can prepare us for the infinite, and the silence, and the realisation that we are utterly on our own.

We'll need to find ways to cope. Music helps, books and movies too. Dom likes to play guitar and keeps a Bible in his compartment, but when I asked him about it, he expressed uncertainty in his faith. Shane favours TV series, especially comedies he grew up watching, like *The Simpsons* and *Father Ted*. 'They're comforting,' he told me. 'Reminds me of after-school telly. When these two shows were on, it was the only time my brothers and I didn't fight for the remote.'

Lucia plays chess, sometimes with Dom or me, sometimes with A-T. She's made much progress, over the past year. I suspect by the end of year two she'll be better than even Dom.

As for me, I read a lot, but find it hard to engage for more than half an hour at a time. I especially like to revisit the books I loved as a child or teenager, which are easy to read, and which I see anew. Last week, I reread *Lord of the Flies*.

Anything, really, to bring us back to Earth – to remind us that it is there, bustling with life, waiting for our return.

2

After reading the note that held her name, I rode my bike to see Philly again. She was sat in front of Mrs Tan's house in a cross-legged position that made me think she had been there for a while, waiting for me. When I reached her she stayed seated, challenging me with her stare. 'You can never use it,' she said. 'My full name, I mean. It's only for you to have. Not to say.'

'Okay, I said. 'I promise.'

For the rest of the week I'd meet her there in the morning, and we'd spend the day in Mrs Tan's garden. When it grew too hot we'd shelter under the sycamore, and Philly would show me pages of her book, or we would doze. It felt as if we, as a pair, existed solely in that garden, like a painting whose subjects are held only inside its frame. Which is why, I think, I was so nervous when she came to my house for the first time. It felt like we were transgressing a rule, a law that governed our new friendship.

In the morning we were at Mrs Tan's. She had prepared sandwiches for lunch, chicken and cucumber, and Philly and I ate them in the garden. I picked the crumbs from my plate. I was always hungry, back then.

'Here,' Philly said, lifting half a sandwich from her plate. 'You can have mine.'

'No, no,' I said. 'It's yours.'

'I can see you eyeing it. Go on, it's okay. I don't like sandwiches very much.'

'Really?' I said. I took her last triangle.

'No. I have them all the time back home. My parents sell sandwiches in their shop. They go bad after a day, so we have to eat them, if they don't sell. Or they go to waste.'

I imagined her house, piles of unwanted sandwiches up to the ceiling, growing staler by the day, until they were nothing but a mountain of mouldy bread.

When we had finished eating, Philly suggested it was time we looked for the cicadas elsewhere.

'I can hear them so well,' she said. 'They must be nearby.' We both knew what this implied: that we should go and explore Joe Harding's fields. They were endless, rows and rows of golden wheat or rapeseed, stretching far beyond what our eyes could see. In the middle of the fields there was a birch, a patch of green in the blue sky, casting a shadow across the wheat. Philly gazed at it, magnifier still in her hand. 'They must be nearby,' she repeated.

All the children in the village were frightened of Joe Harding. He seemed, to me, about a hundred years old: his face was made up of wrinkles and not much else, thin lips and eyes an uncanny grey. Sometimes we'd spot him in the village, walking back from the shop or hunched over a pint in the back room of the Shield, always on his own. But mostly his existence was to us that of a mythical creature, residing half in obscurity and half in our imagination. There were rumours that once he'd caught Jimmy Lovett's brother and his friends frightening his sheep, and when they got home they had red eyes and legs covered with bruises. That he slept with a shotgun under his pillow, aiming it at any bird or fox he caught rummaging through his crops. And that in his garage he held, like trophies, a collection of all the footballs that children had inadvertently kicked into his field, never to be reclaimed.

'You know,' I said, sheepishly, 'I hear them near my house, too, I think.'

We cycled across the village. I worried about anything that might go wrong. Would my old pants and socks be hanging on the line in the garden? Would Mum call me one of her embarrassing nicknames, topping it off with a kiss on the forehead? I cycled faster, hoping that if I got there before Philly I could prevent any humiliations befalling me. I battled against the wind, but she caught up with me, no trouble.

I opened the front door slowly and dramatically, Philly close behind. My mother was lounging on the sofa doing the crossword, listening to the radio. She was a French teacher at the school so my summer holidays were also hers. 'Hello there,' she said, getting up from the sofa. 'You must be Philly. Ollie's told us so much about you. How's your aunt?' I gave her a look that was half-annoyed, half-pleading with her to stop talking. I peeked at the garden, which to my relief was empty of laundry. Mum grinned at me. 'I'll get you two some orange juice. Ollie, you should show Philly your room before you go outside again. You need to cool down, both of you.'

We went up the stairs and into my bedroom. 'Well,' I said, with a lack of enthusiasm that masked nervousness. 'Here it is.' I showed Philly my superheroes, my Game Boy and my books, but only my walls caught her attention. A couple of years before, my parents had asked me to pick the wallpaper. I'd flipped through the pages of the catalogue, passing dinosaurs and racing cars and farm animals, until one caught my eye. It was of our galaxy, with hand-drawn stars, planets and rockets. 'That one,' I said, unable to explain why it had called to me, and the galaxy ended up plastered to my wall. No doubt it became useful later on, as everyone loves a good origin story. Before the

PHOENIX launch, *Time* had written a profile of me, which began with the rather grand sentence: 'Commander Oliver Ines grew up in a bedroom covered with shining stars and planets – filling his nights with dreams of our galaxy, and the countless mysteries it holds.'

What I loved most about the space wallpaper, was that it was glow-in-the-dark. My parents plastered it all over, even on the ceiling, and when I went to sleep the planets and the stars pierced the darkness, bright dots surrounding me – and if you played along, if you gave way to your imagination, you could think they were real. Wanting to show Philly, I pulled my window blinds down, and the walls shone faintly.

'It's better when it's fully dark,' I explained, disappointed by the dimness.

'No,' she said. 'I like it like that.' She peered around the room, observing the planets the same way she observed the grass in the garden – as if they revealed things to her to which I wasn't privy. After a while she lay down on the floor, taking in the gleaming ceiling. I went and sat next to her.

Around that summer, there was a song you couldn't escape, 'Unchained Melody' by Robson & Jerome. I wasn't that fond of it, but it was one of Mum's favourites. We had the CD, and when she drove me to and from football practice or parties, she'd play it in the car, like when she came to pick me up from Jimmy Lovett's birthday. His family lived on a farm about a fifteen-minute drive from the village, and invites to his parties were very much sought-after. You could take turns playing with some of the animals, and his parents would organise a sack race and an egg-and-spoon race, and inside the barn they would lay out an extravagant buffet of sweets and birthday cakes.

I'd been happily surprised when Jimmy handed me an invitation for his ninth birthday. We weren't particularly close then. It wasn't until we went to Imperial together that we bonded, but I'd taken the invite as a sign that he wanted us to be friends or, at least, that as the two top students, he held some sort of appreciation towards me.

The details of the party have very much faded. I only remember that it passed by in a joyful blur, all of us in high spirits and in a sugary trance. It wasn't until near the end that my mood shifted. The farm was emptying of children and Jimmy's mother cleared the table while I hung nearby. 'Have you had a good time, Ollie?' she said. 'We're so glad you came. Your mum's always been such a lovely teacher to Jimmy, Laura and Jack.'

I knew she had meant no harm by this. No doubt it wouldn't even have crossed her mind. Yet her words left me feeling as desolate as the paper plates she was collecting, torn and with half-eaten slices of cake and juice stains. I realised I hadn't been invited because Jimmy wished to be my friend, nor because he held me in high regards, but because my mother was his and his siblings' teacher. I watched as Jimmy's mum disposed of the plates in the giant bin bag, and soon after my mum came to collect me.

'Did the Lovetts' cat get your tongue, Ollie?' Mum said, during the car ride back. 'Jimmy's mum said you all had a great time.' I didn't answer. How could I explain to her the embarrassment she had inadvertently caused? I rested my head on the back seat, alone with my sullen thoughts, as she observed me from the rear-view mirror. It was before dusk, a breeze coming in through my window, and 'Unchained Melody' came on. Mum slowed the car and turned up the volume, and she began to sing along.

The orange sun was reaching the horizon in front of us so that looking in her direction blinded me, yet my eyes were fixed on her. She sang in an overly dramatic way to make me laugh, her curls golden and almost red in the light. She had one hand on the wheel and with the other she reached for my palm, using it as an imaginary mic. I did my best to keep my straight face, but within seconds I was laughing and singing with her, even though I could see people in other cars glaring at us, even though I could barely see her through the rays of the setting sun.

As Philly and I lay on my bedroom floor, the song came on the radio. But this time it was a different version, an older-sounding one by the Righteous Brothers that I'd never heard before. And maybe it was lying there with Philly, or the wistfulness in the singer's voice and the lulling melody of the piano; maybe it was the eeriness of that particular version being played right at that moment, but as the song infused the room, it filled it with a melancholic longing that enthralled me.

The song continued, and underneath it I could hear Philly breathing and my own heart thumping, our legs brushing against the tired carpet. I had the urge to reach for her hand, as I'd seen the leads do in my favourite films. I began lifting my fingers, but I thought that any further movement would break the delicate stillness that held us. I sank them back into the carpet, and our hands lingered there, a few inches from one another, for what was probably only a minute but, in my mind, stretched much longer.

———

This morning on *Talos*, after breakfast, I cleaned the air filters with my headphones on. There was a bit of dust, some hair and lint and a few crumbs, and as I vacuumed them up, the familiar notes invaded my ears. I didn't even know I had it saved on my audio player, yet there it was. I let go of the hoover in surprise, and a wave of emotion washed over me. Shane was in the control room and Lucia and Dom were busy so I was alone on the deck, my hand clinging to the rail, the vacuum gently drifting by the vent.

I've been gone for almost five years, cut off from the world, birthdays and Christmases, gone without so much as a call from Earth. Yet I've never felt quite like this. It was as if everything I had lost collapsed over me at once, and all I could do was let it submerge me completely, until I was nothing but those losses. I wasn't crying because I missed home, but rather for all the days gone by. For the years I hadn't seen pass but that now flooded the room like ghosts. I mourned that young boy and girl, whose biggest worry was whether they should reach for each other's hand as they lay on the carpet, staring at the ceiling.

PHOENIX MISSION
Commander Oliver Ines's Personal Log

Talos, Day 812. Earth is now a faint dot.

It was Easter Sunday yesterday. It's always the holidays that are the hardest. I'm dreading Mother's Day that's coming up.

Like last year, I woke up early, trying not to disturb the rest of the crew. I spent about an hour hiding chocolate eggs across *Talos* – three for each of them, one for me. It's harder than one might think. I had to handle the tape with one hand, tearing it off with my teeth, while holding the eggs in place with the other. Overall, I think I did a reasonably good job. I taped some behind Lucia's microscope, planted one in our potato field (which appears a bit sad, these days – I'll ask Lucia to look into it), behind the fridge, on top of our lockers. When I'd finished, I counted how many eggs we had left in store: there should be enough to last another two Easters, or three, if I ration them more carefully.

I think they were happy to have the egg hunt. What a strange sight to see Dom, Shane and Lucia – two pilots, one physicist – acting like kids again, eggs escaping from their hands as they chased after them. Even Lucia, who's been missing her family (next week is the anniversary of her father's death, which I must mark), seemed to appreciate the distraction. Once we were all done, Dom came up behind me, patting me on the back. He put one of the eggs into his mouth and savoured it slowly.

'Three hundred and sixty-five days till the next one,' he said.

Perhaps I should have brought more eggs on board.

3

By August of that summer, the Mini looked as good as new. To celebrate, my father took me for a ride around the village, all the way to the railway and back, and parked at the Shield. We sat by the bar, my feet hovering over the floor, as Dad ordered an apple juice and a beer. He passed his glass to me. 'Come on, you can have a taste,' he said, and I had my first sip of beer, the bitterness and the cold sharp on my tongue.

'I like it,' I told him, lying, but he seemed pleased. We drank in silence for a while, unsure of what to say. We weren't used to spending time just the two of us. When we did, it was usually in the garage, without much room for conversation.

He tapped his glass with his fingers in a rhythmic pattern, as we turned our attention to Gerry the barman, pulling pints. 'You did well with that car,' Dad said.

'Thank you, 'I said. 'I had a good time. Doing the repairs, I mean.'

'Good,' he said. 'I'm glad.' The morning service had

ended. Churchgoers flowed into the pub, cooling themselves as best they could. 'You could do more,' Dad continued.

I waited for a second, thinking he might go on. 'You mean, with you?' I said, when he didn't.

'No. Well, why not? But I meant that you could make a good living out of it later. It's what I would have done, if . . . well, if I'd had the chance, I suppose.'

'A mechanic?' I asked.

'An engineer,' he said. 'Mechanical engineer.' He saw my blank face, turned over his words, and continued: 'You design, you build things. You dream up a machine – car, plane, microwave, anything – and then you make them a reality.' He pointed at the bar. 'See that beer tap? It's made of steel, brass. It's got a shank that connects the keg to the tap. It's got a handle that Gerry pulls to open it. All those elements, you work them all up, all the moving pieces, and you manage to make them, together, greater than the sum of their parts.'

I had the feeling he wasn't really talking to me – more to a faraway version of himself. I observed his profile, his clean-shaven face, his blue-grey eyes that I was told resembled mine. 'That sounds nice,' I said softly.

'Yeah,' he said. 'It does, doesn't it? I'd have liked to do that.'

The pub was now almost full, making it hard for us to

hear one another. The smell of beer and roasting meats began to overwhelm the room. Mr and Mrs Burns, who lived next door, came to greet us. Afterwards, Dad finished his beer in one gulp. 'Come on,' he said. 'We can't make your mum wait for lunch.'

I jumped down from the stool, my juice glass half-full, and followed him to the car. He was quiet on the short ride back, muttering to himself about the churchgoers lingering in the car park. In my mind I replayed what he had said. I stored his words away carefully, I let them simmer in my nine-year-old self, and slowly I digested them into something more: that engineers were builders of dreams.

4

The next day Mrs Tan asked Philly and me to run an errand in the town, which had a supermarket. On our way I told Philly about the ride in the Mini and the beer, but not the engineer talk: it had been one of those conversations that I intuitively knew belonged only to its speakers.

'What did it taste like?' she asked, about the beer. 'My dad let me try the foam once. But I couldn't really taste anything.'

'Bitter,' I said. 'But not in a bad way. Also, a little sweet . . . like honey, almost.'

She thought this over. 'When you're an adult, do you think you'll go to the Shield? To drink beers with friends?'

'Yes,' I said. 'That's what grown-ups do, isn't it?'

'I think so,' she said, unsure of herself. 'But do you think they *like* doing it? Or is it just a – a thing to do? I mean, when does it stop becoming fun, everything that *we* do? The garden, your figurines and all that. Do you think we'll wake up one day, and all these things won't be fun anymore?'

'Maybe when you become an adult you lose interest in that stuff. Like, maybe you don't even realise it.'

'But what if you don't want to?' she persisted. 'Can you stop it happening?'

'I don't know,' I said. 'We'll just have to see, right?'

'I guess so. But it's weird, how no one talks about it. How it just happens.'

'Yeah,' I said. 'It is kind of weird.'

We arrived at the eastern side of the village, where the railway was located. It was enclosed by wire fences but they were battered and low, only half our size. There were signs everywhere forbidding trespassing and warning of the danger of death. Yet children would often cut across the track to reach a field that led directly to the neighbouring town.

Traversing the track had become a kind of trial for the children of the village. If you crossed you were bold and worthy, and if you took the long way, through muddy grounds that added an extra fifteen minutes to your walk, you were neither of those things. And after all, what was the harm? The railway was rarely in use and you could see and hear incoming trains from miles away. Without thinking, I began to climb the fence.

'What are you doing?' Philly said. 'It says we're not allowed.'

I stopped and jumped down. I tried to explain the shortcut to her.

'But it says we're not allowed.'

'I know. But it's okay. I do it all the time, don't worry.'

'I'm not worried,' she said. 'But we're not in a hurry, are we?'

'It's what all my friends do,' I said. 'Only the smaller kids take the long way.'

She stared at me, wide-eyed, as if my words evaded a logic so obvious they came out as alien. 'But they're not here, your friends. It's just me. And I don't take that shortcut. It's not worth it. It's silly.'

Everything she said made sense, but I was reluctant to let the matter go. We stood motionless, neither of us wanting to start an argument or to concede. Her gaze didn't let go of mine, a hint of defiance in it. I pinched my lips tightly, hesitant. After a minute or two, not wanting to make any more of a fuss, I shrugged, glanced at the fence one last time, and led us the long way round.

It was only much later that I was able to sum up what had bothered me so much about our standstill. For me, the railway was more than a crossing. It was proof I was brave, that I was daring and unafraid, and when I crossed it, I did so with that bigger picture in mind. Philly, on the other hand, saw crossing it for what it was at face value: a reckless, pointless act. We were talking at cross purposes, but back then, I hadn't given it too much weight. And maybe that's why I've been thinking about that summer lately. I'm trying to make sense of all those innocuous moments. Of the little things I missed that seemed of no importance but, in truth, were harbingers of all that was to come.

We walked alongside the railway, mostly in silence. The fields were parched, the dry grass pricking my ankles, and they were strangely empty. The heat wave was nearing its end, the wind carrying the promise of rain, the whole village holding its breath for the downpour. Philly trudged ahead in the field, her fingers stroking the wheat as I lingered behind.

After we had visited the shop and were nearing the village again, I asked if she wanted to come to my house. 'I could show you the Mini,' I said. 'The one my dad and I repaired.'

'I can't,' she said. She fiddled with the hem of her dress, while I hid my disappointment. 'I told Auntie Mel I'd be back soon. I've got to pack my bags.'

'Where are you going?' I asked.

'Home,' she said. 'I . . . I was going to tell you. My parents, they're coming to pick me up tomorrow morning.'

'Oh.'

'Yes,' she said, and then, more brightly, she added, 'but I'll be back next summer.'

'Okay,' I said. 'So . . . I'll see you then?'

'Yes,' she said. She hesitated an instant. 'You won't look

for them without me, will you? The cicadas, I mean. You'll wait for me, right?'

'Of course,' I said. 'I'll wait for you.'

The heat wave broke that evening and there was a thunderstorm all through the night. I stayed wide awake, staring up at the planets and stars on my walls, lightning occasionally bathing my room in brightness. I leapt out of bed before dawn and got dressed. By the time I reached Mrs Tan's, her front door was open, and Philly's dad was carrying her luggage to the car. I stood on the other side of the road, half-hidden behind the corner of a neighbouring house. The air was fresh, and the smell of wet grass coursed through the village.

'We've got to go, Philly,' her mother called impatiently, 'or we'll get stuck in traffic.'

'Coming, Mum,' I heard Philly say. She walked out from the front door slowly and frowning. She hugged Mrs Tan goodbye, and when she got into the car I saw her glance around a final time, carefully. I took one last look at her, her dark hair in a plait, her favourite yellow dress stained with grass, her large eyes darting around, as if to spot something. It was not quite daylight, and the fields were yet to be illuminated – but before she disappeared into the car, I thought I caught a flash of disappointment cross her face. I felt a pang of sadness, because of her leaving, yes, but that wasn't all. I saw her standing there, adults rushing her about, her small frame about to be engulfed by the car, and I saw that she was lonely. And I knew that I had only been able to perceive this because I had recognised in her loneliness something of my own.

'Are you alright, Ollie?' Mum asked me at breakfast. She had tanned over the summer, and freckles had appeared on her nose and cheeks. She was not fully awake, and she started making coffee drowsily, pouring hot water over the filter.

'Yes,' I said. 'I'm okay.' I sat at the table and reached for the milk and cereal. Outside, it was raining again. I watched the raindrops falling down the window, as if racing to the bottom. I sensed Mum observing me. 'Philly went home this morning,' I said, in a tone I meant to sound casual.

'Oh, darling, I'm sorry,' she said. 'You two got along well, didn't you?'

I gave a feeble nod, a tightness building in my throat. To give myself something to do, I went to fetch the orange juice from the fridge. When I sat back down, she pulled my bowl of cereal away. 'I'll tell you what,' she said, with the knowing smile she reserved for mischief. 'It's the holidays, isn't it? Why don't we have ice cream? As a special treat.'

'For breakfast?' I asked. 'Can we do that?'

'Not every day,' she said. 'But sometimes, on very special days, yes. We can.'

She got the chocolate mint ice cream out of the fridge and scooped two large spheres into a bowl. I got two spoons from the drawer. 'Just don't tell your dad, okay?'

We took turns diving into the bowl, the freshness of the mint livening me at once.

'See?' Mum said. 'Isn't it nice, to start your day like this?'

I nodded, taking another mouthful. I knew she was trying to cheer me up, and while another time I might have refused to play along, that day I remember feeling grateful, and I remember feeling loved. 'Here,' I said, passing her the bowl. 'You have the last spoonful.'

At the end of the summer, Joe Harding passed away in his sleep. His death disturbed me. It seemed to take not only his person but all the myths that surrounded him, all the stories for which he was feared and renowned, revealing him to be an ordinary man. I couldn't help but imagine him alone in his bed, his breathing slowing to a whisper, coming to a complete halt. Yet the village and the world kept going as if nothing had happened; as if his death and his life had been nothing but dust that had already been wiped away. And I imagined that perhaps he kept our footballs in his garage not as trophies, but rather in the hope that one day we would come knocking at his door to ask for them back.

It all happened quickly afterwards. Joe's farm was passed on to a nephew of his, who in turn sold it to a property developer, who spoke finely and wore a suit and looked out of place in the village. Wanting to buy parcels of land throughout the area, in the winter he made an offer to Mrs Tan for her property. 'A generous offer, very generous,' she told my parents, when she came over for tea. She was thrilled. She explained that she would use the money to go abroad, and to move closer to her children who had settled in London. I didn't ask her about Philly. In the months since I'd last seen her, I'd convinced myself that that summer had been nothing but two children trying to pass the time. I had not grasped yet how important she was to me. I had not realised that those years in which we lost touch held thousands of vanished moments between us – of memories that could have been, which I could have carried with me to *Talos*.

The following summer, Mrs Tan's house was demolished and the garden torn up. All the roses were razed, their sweet fragrance lingering for weeks. In the end, only the sycamore remained standing, its branches reaching out into the emptiness.

PHOENIX MISSION
Commander Oliver Ines's Personal Log

Talos, Day 1104. Earth is no longer visible.

I've found that the best way to help with morale is to keep everyone busy, so I've increased our time on the treadmill to three hours a day. I've given the crew innocuous tasks: count the food and med supplies (we're running low on painkillers, which I need to investigate), till the soil of the potato field (which is thriving, thanks to Lucia), tidy the housekeeping deck, or do some pilot training on the VR headset. No doubt they're aware of what I'm doing, but they don't complain. I think they're grateful, really.

Shane, who I usually rely on to brighten everyone's day, has been a little quiet. Yesterday, over breakfast, he asked, 'What do you think Philly and Liv are doing now?' He seemed more tired than ever. He had dark rings under his eyes and I noticed, for the first time, that his messy red hair had streaks of grey. I pictured the boyish, brash and vigorous version of him I'd first come across twenty-odd years ago. Today, that Shane appeared very far away, which troubled me. He grabbed a pouch of porridge and powdered milk and went to the rehydration station.

'Well,' I said. 'It's about eight o'clock in London now so Philly is probably having breakfast with Tommy. It's a Thursday, so she'll be taking him to school in about twenty minutes.' He put the pouch into the food warmer. I went on: 'They'll be running late, and rushing out of the door, as usual.' That image made me smile, and I stayed in it for a moment. I imagined Philly wrapping Tommy in his teddy bear coat, until I remembered he had surely outgrown it by now, and that I didn't know what coat he currently wore. Shane untaped his spoon and began eating his porridge. Lucia and Dom came in.

'What's wrong, Shane?' Dom said. 'Not liking your wet-paper paste for breakfast?' Lucia chuckled. I shushed them with my hand. Dom grabbed a granola bar, and made an odd face as he ate it, like a grimace, though I wasn't sure why: it was one of the tastiest we had.

'Lucia,' I said, trying to change the topic. 'Any requests for your birthday tomorrow? What do you want to do?'

'Honestly,' she said, 'nothing. Please.'

'You sure? We'll have those chocolate-cake pouches. And we can watch that movie you like. What was it again?'

'*Before Sunrise?*'

'Oh, my God,' Shane said. 'Please, no. Not again. That was the worst two hours of my life.'

'Don't worry,' Lucia said, laughing. 'I mean it. I'd rather we treat tomorrow like a normal day. It's just so depressing, trying to make it special, you know? Makes you more aware of all the ways you can't celebrate it.'

'What would you normally do?' Dom asked.

'Nothing crazy. Probably spend the day with some friends. Maybe go to the movies, have some drinks by the canals. In the evening, I'd go to my mum's and we'd have cake and I'd blow out the candles and make a wish. And then who knows? Maybe I'd meet my friends again and we'd go out and dance and flirt and drink some more.'

None of us said anything. I suppose we were all picturing Lucia's day, inserting ourselves in it.

'Yep,' Dom said. 'Can't do any of that up here, I'm afraid.'

'Can I ask,' Shane said, 'and I'm only asking out of pure curiosity, nothing more. I won't judge your answers, and I don't think anyone else should either.' He paused, choosing his words carefully. 'But if you were to start again, with the knowledge of what it's like here, would you maybe – and again, I don't think there's a right or wrong answer here – would you maybe reconsider joining this mission?'

No one wanted to be the first to answer. And I felt that, as commander, I should listen rather than speak. A bit of Shane's porridge floated out of his spoon and hung there for an instant, until he grabbed it with his mouth. Finally, Lucia took the lead.

'It's hard. I miss my family. I miss jogging in the park and going swimming and having a drink with my girlfriends and all those things I used to take for granted.' She paused. 'I miss having a fucking shower. But to answer your question, no, I don't regret coming here. What we're doing, it's beyond any of us. It's beyond our comfort and longings.' She looked at Dom and me for support.

'In a hundred years' time, people will know what we did,' I said, trying to convey a sense of assurance. 'We're going further, longer into the galaxy, than anyone else before us. There'll be books and documentaries about us. About how we defied science, the crucial part we played in its progress, and in our understanding of the universe.' They waited for me to go on. I could tell they wanted dearly to believe me. 'And that,' I concluded, 'is worth some personal sacrifices.'

Lucia and Dom nodded. Shane stared at his porridge. 'I suppose you're right,' he said, after a while. 'I suppose you're right.' I relaxed my stance, somewhat relieved no one wished to continue the conversation.

Shane finished his meal, cleaned up and went back to the control room. I'll keep an eye on him this week and try my best to lift his mood. It's unusual for him to act like that. But I really do think the best way to help with morale is to keep everyone busy, away from the lurking blues, so I'll continue to give him and the rest of the crew some tasks to complete.

5

I never asked Jimmy Lovett why he applied for the same university course as me. Only a few in our class went on to further education. Most of our classmates took apprenticeships or got jobs, and Jimmy's siblings joined their parents at their farm. I suppose I might have served as some sort of inspiration, or maybe it was simply that mechanical engineering was considered one of the best degrees for students who were good at maths and physics, like us. In any case, I was glad to have a familiar face in London when I moved there in 2004 to attend Imperial.

We had one seminar together in our first year, Fluid Mechanics. It was taught by Professor Whitley, a man in his fifties, early sixties perhaps, always wearing a brown jacket and trousers that were both just a little too big for him, and brightly coloured ties. He had a way of speaking that could transform even the grimmest equation into something that resembled a miracle, and during his office hours on Wednesdays, the queue would run all along the corridor of the third floor.

For his seminars, we had to arrange the tables in a circle so that there was no head and no hierarchy, like the Knights of the Round Table. We'd sit there, a dozen of us, and discuss that week's lecture, or go through some problems in groups of two or three. I didn't care for the circle. I didn't like how exposed it made me feel, all eyes on me, my eyes on everyone else. Discussion was always free-ranging in his class, and it wasn't unusual for seminars to wander off to topics only loosely related to the syllabus. In one of our first lessons, about entropy, we sidetracked to discussing the EROS mission, which was due to launch imminently.

It was all most of us could talk about: the first time humans were to land on Mars, in a NASA- and JAXA-funded mission. Commander Hatsuo Masuda had been on *Late Show with David Letterman* a couple of nights before, and they'd replayed the interview on ITV. He was in his late thirties, with sharp, handsome features. He had a quiet intensity about him, which drew Letterman and the audience closer. He talked about the mission, and his upbringing in a village near Kyoto, which hadn't seemed so dissimilar to mine.

One thing he said in particular struck me. Letterman asked him, 'How do you feel, leaving your home, leaving Earth, leaving everything, really, for almost four years?' Maybe it wasn't worded exactly like that, but it was very much in that vein. The audience fell quiet. I was watching the telly from the communal area of my halls, which I shared with five other students. I often spent time in there because my bedroom was split with an anthropology student I disliked. He had a habit of leaving piles of dirty mugs and bowls on his desk, which gave the room a musty smell, and he slept throughout the day, so that I'd have to spend most of my time tiptoeing around him.

Joy and Arthur were in the common room as well, and all three of us bent towards the screen, awaiting Masuda's response. I suppose what we expected, what we all wanted from him, was an answer that was deep and meaningful. An answer that would point to a greater purpose, a momentous reason that would warrant such sacrifices. But Masuda merely shrugged and gave a playful smile, as if he found the question amusing. And then, in an English that had Japanese inflections but remained perfectly clear, he said, 'It's just part of the job.'

Back in Professor Whitley's seminar, all the students talked enthusiastically about Masuda and about the mission, and then Lea Mann, one of the prettiest and cleverest girls in the year, raised her hand. 'What about the environmental cost, though? Hundred tons of CO_2 emissions, from the lift-off alone. Can we really justify the damage done to our planet?' The room erupted in chatter.

Jimmy – I was always amazed by how easily he took the floor – brought up utilitarianism, and argued that, on the whole, the huge costs were worth it since the mission's benefits outweighed them. 'Think about what its geology could teach us,' he said. 'You heard what Masuda said. The mission's findings will tell us so much about the origins and the future of life on Earth.'

A murmur of approval pervaded the room. 'Yeah, but who is really benefiting, though?' Lea said. 'Can we really say that going to Mars will improve the majority of people's quality of life in any demonstrable way?'

Our circle went silent. I was scribbling in my notebook, trying not to get myself noticed. Professor Whitley always liked to pick on quiet students, and while at school I hadn't been one of the quiet ones, here it was different: it felt like everyone had had access to some secret manual unavailable to me that taught them how to debate and act and all the right things there were to know. I knew about the EROS mission, yes, but I didn't know much about the environmental costs or philosophical doctrines and how they related to one another. I scribbled away, but of course Professor Whitley's voice rose: 'What do you think, Oliver?'

I glanced up from my notes. The whole circle turned towards me expectantly. Jimmy gave me a nod of support, and I felt Lea's blue eyes on me. I shuffled in my seat, my fingers gripping my pen. I can't remember what I said exactly – only that it was an unremarkable answer, which assured the class that I could see both sides of the argument and that mitigating environmental risk was important, while failing to give any real judgement or insight. Professor Whitley observed me for an instant, waiting to see if I would continue. I felt the heat rushing to my cheeks. 'Well,' he said, finally. 'Let's move on now, shall we?'

After Masuda spoke, Letterman, the audience, all of us watching, waited for him to clarify what he'd meant. 'Just part of the job?' Letterman repeated, perhaps thinking something had been lost in translation. 'Well, I'll tell you what, if CBS asked me to do that, I'd be outta here in a jiff.' The audience laughed, Masuda smiled politely again, and Letterman wrapped up the interview. Joy and Arthur got up from the sofa, and I was left alone in the lounge, pondering the banality of his answer.

6

Not long after that seminar, I travelled home for Reading Week. My parents came to pick me up from the station. I sat in the back of the car, as I had many times before, but when I watched the village course through my window, I did so through different eyes. Its smallness surprised me. We passed by the houses and the bungalows, and I thought of my student halls, fifteen storeys high, the overarching view of London its roof terrace offered. We passed by the church, the tallest building in the village that had seemed, as a child, so colossal, so supreme, and I realised that it was half the size of my lecture theatres. Even the smell of our house, a floral, old-fashioned smell I'd never paid any attention to, appeared new to me. It reached me as soon as I crossed the threshold, entering a home that was both mine and foreign.

I went out for a bike ride. The harvests had wound down for the year, and the fields were sparse and grey. I ran into Mrs Burns and Gerry, each asking how I was getting on in London and with my studies. I told them it was all going well, thank you, clasping my bike handlebars tightly. I waited for the conversation to end with an impatience that hadn't been there previously. Gerry expressed worry at how expensive London must be. 'If you ever need a bit of pocket money, you can always take some shifts down at the Shield when you come back to visit.' I assumed he was insinuating that I wouldn't be able to make it on my own in the city, that he was trying to pull me back and tie me to the village. Mrs Burns said she had a nephew in London I could contact anytime, should I need anything – and again I understood that she was doubting me, that she wanted to keep tabs on me, that wherever I went the village's prying eyes would always follow.

I rode past Mrs Tan's old property, which had been turned into a neat row of bungalows, most of them vacant. I contemplated the sycamore, still in their midst. Its leaves had not yet fallen, and from a distance it looked as if it was aflame. The air was heavy with memories. I pictured myself on my bike a decade before, riding across the village. I pictured myself sitting underneath that tree, its leaves shading me from the heat, combing the grass with an odd girl my age called Philly.

It had been a while since she'd popped into my mind. Whenever she did, I always wondered if she had been real, or an imaginary friend I had made up to fill the empty summer days. I had no pictures of her, not even a last name – only the outline of a sweet and curious face, crouched with a magnifying glass as big as her hands. I thought of the warming glow that accompanied her presence, but the singularity of it only made more acute the dullness of these days: her brightness came to me, as a reminder of a lonely world. I surveyed the empty fields behind the bungalows. I had the urge to ride somewhere far away, past the houses and the fields, a place that was empty of memories, where I could create myself anew.

In the afternoon, I sat in the kitchen with Mum. 'So, how's it all going?' she asked. 'You've barely said anything since you got here.'

I focused on the tiles above the stove, a dusty pink with an ornate pattern, their edges feathered with cracks. 'You know,' I said, 'I think this kitchen's starting to feel a bit old, Mum. I could help you get rid of those tiles, if you'd like. We could replace them with something else.'

'Alright, London boy,' she said, amused. 'Sorry our kitchen isn't cool enough for you.'

'That's not what I meant,' I said.

Her expression tightened. I wasn't sure if I had hurt her feelings. 'You're probably right,' she said. 'I've been telling your dad the same. But, well, you know how he is. If it's not falling apart, he doesn't see the point in changing it. Except for cars, of course.'

'Yeah,' I said. 'I know.'

We sat there in silence, waiting for our tea to cool. I looked down at my mug, warming my hands with it, and I sensed Mum's eyes on me again.

'So, you're really not going to tell me how uni's going?'

'There's not much to say. I guess at school I was doing well, wasn't I? I thought it'd be the same in London. That I was one of the clever ones, or whatever. But . . . well, I don't know. It doesn't feel like that anymore. More the opposite, really. Everyone's so eloquent. So good at arguing and all that. Even Jimmy. I wish I could be like that. That I could be somebody else, someone cleverer. I just feel stupid, most of the time.'

'You *are* clever, Ollie,' she said.

'Not really. I was a big fish in a small pond, that's all. I wasn't, like, special or gifted or anything.'

She sighed and sat back in her chair. 'You know, there's an expression in French I really like. It goes, "Knowledge is like jam: the less you have, the more you spread it."' She let go of her mug and grabbed my hands, holding them with a firmness that surprised me. 'If you listen carefully to what most of the loud students are saying, I'm sure you'll realise it's not half as clever as it sounds.'

'I don't know,' I said. 'At least they *have* jam.'

'You do, too,' she said, laughing. 'Buckets of it. You're just not a show-off, that's all. You'll see.'

'Well, of course you'd say that,' I said, a sudden impatience in my voice. 'You're my mum.' I got up briskly, took my tea up to my room, leaving her alone in the kitchen.

How to explain the irritability that came over me during that trip? I felt stifled by everyone's curiosity, by everyone in the village knowing my name, who my parents were and what I had been like as a child. Time can distort events, but it can just as well bend them back into shape – and I recognise now that I had experienced everything that week through a tainted lens. I'd taken my mum's reassuring words for condescending pity. I'd taken Gerry and Mrs Burns's kindness for nosiness, my curtness leaving me with a vague sense of remorse that only increased my frustration towards them, towards the village as a whole. I felt sure they viewed me in a way that I didn't want to be seen. That they had the certainty of knowing who I was, when I was trying to work it out for myself. And perhaps this was all true – but what I had failed to see was that, besides all else, their view of me was wrapped in care.

―――

When I got back to London, I embraced the sense of anonymity it offered. My week at home had troubled me, yes, and to keep busy I became immersed in my studies. I found comfort in the certainty maths and physics offered, worlds governed by logic, each exercise I solved a validation of my labours. I spent evenings in the library, in a quiet spot I'd found tucked behind the geology section. On Wednesdays I'd queue for Professor Whitley's office hours and became an active participant in his seminars. By the time mid-term exams arrived, I was what you could call a model student – and because I was on top of my workload, I resolved to attend extra lectures from other departments.

I scrolled down the list of modules available to me. I considered doing an economics course, improving my French, or studying post-war English literature. I scrolled further down, nothing really calling my name, until I fell upon a module called 'Stars, Planets and Our Universe'. I thought about trips to the Science Museum and my superheroes battling aliens from faraway galaxies. I pictured my young self fighting off sleep, staring at the planets on his walls and ceiling, brilliant and fake. And I thought how the village had seemed so small that week I had gone to visit, and how this module was about immensity, about all of the great entities that only those who looked upwards could see.

From January, every Thursday morning, I made my way across campus to the wooden lecture theatre, its rows of seats shaped in a half-circle. I'd sit at the back discreetly, not talking to the other students, not drawing any attention to myself. I'd sit there with my notebook, pen in hand, as the universe opened up to me. I learnt about Kepler's Law of Planetary Motion, exoplanets and asteroids, the Kuiper belt and the Oort cloud. I learnt about tidal forces and planetary rings and many other things that I would come to witness with my own eyes.

Halfway through term, we studied Jupiter's Galilean moons: Ganymede's magnetic field, the cratered surface of Callisto, Io's volcanism and, of course, Europa. On the lesson's slides I took in her smooth and icy exterior, as the lecturer told us about the likely ocean buried beneath her surface, more plentiful than all of Earth's seas. I listened attentively as he explained that that ocean may, like our own planet, be a source of life.

We will know soon enough whether that's true or not. Before we do, in only some hundred days, she will come into view. First as a faded speck, then a bright dot, her features sharpening as we near. And finally the day will come, when I'll see Europa as clearly as I had on that slide almost thirty years ago, sat alone at the back of the lecture theatre.

PHOENIX MISSION

Commander Oliver Ines's Personal Log

Talos, Day 1394. We're getting nearer. We can just about see the Great Red Spot now, and it's as if it's staring at us.

'Ollie, what will you say?' Shane asked me, over dinner. It had been a while since we'd had it all together, and the room felt cramped but merry.

'Huh?'

'You know, when we land on Europa. Armstrong's got "One small step for man", Masuda's got "The red planet is not so lonely today." You've got to step up your game. For the history books, remember?' Lucia and Dom snorted.

'I don't know,' I said casually. 'Haven't really thought about it, to be honest.' I ate a bit of my pasta, making sure not to elbow Dom, who was floating near me.

Okay, so maybe I hadn't been completely truthful. I've been having bouts of insomnia lately – probably the excitement of almost reaching the halfway point of our journey – which I've been using to think about my landing words. So far, I've failed to come up with anything striking. 'I was hoping inspiration would hit me on the spot,' I said, to the group.

'Nah,' Shane said. 'That won't do. You gotta be prepared. Dom, Lucia, any suggestions?'

Everyone racked their brains. I smiled internally: it was pleasing to see us all relaxing together like that. Only last month, the atmosphere on board had been much lower.

'How about,' Dom said, after a minute or so, ' "Tonight, Europa has four humble visitors in its kingdom." '

Shane, Lucia and I looked at one another, before bursting out laughing. Bits of food flew out of our trays.

'Oh my God,' Lucia said. 'That's the lamest shit I've ever heard.'

'It's a mythology reference!' Dom said. 'You're all too dumb to get it.'

'Oh no, we're not. We got it,' Shane said. 'We just think it's incredibly uncool.'

'Well, any better suggestions?'

'No,' Lucia said. 'But it's okay. We have what? A year now, to figure it out?'

'Six hundred and eighty-six days before landing,' Shane said.

'Wow,' Lucia said, her voice teeming with irony. 'Time flies when you're having fun.'

A good evening overall, but that begot a serious matter. I'll have to give my landing words a bit more consideration. After all, even if Shane was joking, he wasn't wrong: they'll be the words that define me, long after the mission is over, long after I've gone. The words people will remember me by.

7

In my second year, I moved into a flatshare with three other students from our department: Chelsea, Katie and Ben. I had been hunting for a flat, and they for a fourth flatmate – and while we weren't particularly close, we got along perfectly well. We lived in Kentish Town, in a sixties maisonette that was falling apart, but that was cheap and bright and large enough for the four of us. My room was on the top floor, just big enough for a small desk and a bed, and I liked to spend whole days cooped up in it, reading, watching *Lost*, disappearing from the world. From the window you could see the City, the Gherkin, all those big buildings that make up London's skyline, and I'd imagine myself one day working in one of those skyscrapers. Taking meetings and calls, about what I wasn't sure yet, chatting to colleagues by the photocopier. I didn't know that life would take me somewhere else. I didn't know that my office would be sailing through the Milky Way, at 4,000 miles per hour.

In April, as exam season approached, I spent a Friday

night revising for a computing class. I was feeling fairly confident – none of my classes were giving me too much trouble, but there were two or three formulas I wanted to go over. At about half past nine, I went to the kitchen to get a Red Bull. It was only me in the flat, so I took the opportunity to sit down at the dining table, a plastic one meant for gardens that Ben had found on Gumtree, enjoying the peace. I let my mind wander, to exams coming up, the latest episode of *Lost*, or whatever else I'd been up to that day. I heard the lock rattling in the front door, the laughter of my flatmates coming from the other side.

There was no way for me to leave discreetly: the door stood between the stairs and the kitchen. I figured that if they saw me retreating as they came in, it would seem rude.

'Oh, hi, Ollie,' Katie said, surprised, as she turned into the kitchen.

'Hi,' I said, in a friendly tone.

'We didn't know you were in. We thought . . . well, we thought you were out.'

'No, I stayed in tonight. Got an exam coming up.'

'Oh, I see. I've got a couple in a week as well.'

Chelsea and Ben were watching the scene unfold. They were all trying hard to act sober. Ben passed me and grabbed some beers from the fridge.

'How's your evening?' I asked.

'It was good, thanks,' Katie said. 'Nothing crazy. We had predrinks at Joy's. Do you know Joy? She does physics . . .'

'Yeah,' I said. 'We were in halls together.'

'Oh,' she said. 'I didn't know.'

We talked for a little longer, and then I excused myself and went back to my room and my notebooks. I stared at the formulas I'd written down so carefully, but my zeal for them had vanished. I went to my window. It was a clear night, but the stars were not visible under the London sky. The only lights that pierced it were from the buildings and the cars, and for the first time in a while, something that resembled homesickness came over me. The room, my flatmates, the skyline – I had the odd sensation of not being a part of any of it. As if I were a spectre wandering through those places, not inhabiting them. I checked the time: it was early enough. I texted Jimmy, to see what he was up to. He lived just down the road, in a house even more derelict than ours. While not being especially good friends, we shared a closeness that can only exist from having grown up with someone. He answered quickly. 'Hey, mate, yeah, I'm around,' he said. 'Fancy a drink at the Goldhawk?' That was the pub near ours.

'Great,' I said. 'I'll see you there in ten.'

By the time I got to the pub they were ringing the bell for last orders. I found Jimmy at a table at the back, his blond hair standing out in front of the dark wood-panelled wall. He waved at me. 'Here,' he said. 'I got you a Peroni.'

'Thanks,' I said. 'I'll get you one next time.'

We talked about our classes and our exams. The pub and the streets were emptying so that the room felt progressively quieter, giving our talk unsought intimacy.

'Will you apply for the master's?' he asked me.

'I think so,' I said. 'No harm trying, right?'

'Same. Only if I can get the Ormond Scholarship, though.'

'Right,' I said. 'Me too.' I hid my surprise. Professor Whitley had recently encouraged me to apply for that scholarship. It was offered to two engineering undergraduates at Imperial who wished to go on to further studies, awarded based on a mixture of academic merit and financial need. The grant was substantial enough to cover most living costs for the duration of a master's degree. 'I'm not on the judging panel,' Professor Whitley had told me. 'But I would throw my hat in the ring, if I were you. The department would love to keep you.'

Now that I thought about it, it was only natural for him to give Jimmy the same advice. We were both at the top of our year, and our financial situations were roughly similar. But I suppose it did come as a disappointment, to realise I hadn't been the only one he had encouraged – and I felt foolish for my delusion.

'I'll never get over how expensive everything is here,' Jimmy continued. He pointed at our glasses. 'Six quid for two pints!'

'Oof,' I said. I tilted my glass. 'Thanks again, Jimmy.'

He laughed – the same, high-pitched cackle he'd had as a child. 'You know you're the only one here who calls me that, right? I go by Jamie, now.'

'Oh,' I said. 'I'm sorry. Old habits.'

'Don't worry about it. I don't mind. It just makes me chuckle, that's all.'

The barmen were now stacking chairs on top of the tables, shooting us the occasional glance, making no secret of their desire for us to leave. We finished our drinks, put on our jackets and left the Goldhawk.

'Do you miss it?' he asked. 'Home, I mean.'

'Not really.' I considered telling him about my earlier homesickness, but decided not to. 'I feel like I was pretty much ready to leave, at eighteen.'

'Me too,' he said. We walked in silence for a little bit. The temperature had dropped suddenly over the week, so we were shivering in our jackets. 'But I guess sometimes I do miss it, you know.' He waited for me to say something. It was close to a full moon so that the night had a soft glow, and I could see his face plainly. 'Back then,' he continued, 'it felt like the village was too small to hold my ambition. Like, I was meant for bigger things. I know that sounds conceited, but that's what we were meant to believe at school, right? That if we were studious, or whatever, we should leave. We should go to uni and get a job in the city.'

'Yeah,' I said. 'I felt the same way.'

'But sometimes, when I go back, I see my siblings on the farm, or I see some of our old classmates, and they seem pretty content. You remember Daniel Wilson? He always got terrible grades. I was so scared of ending up like him, bottom of the class, no real prospects. But I ran into him last time I went back. He's working as a builder. Got a nice house in the town, a girl and everything.'

'Really?' I said. I had felt similarly about Daniel. 'Good for him.'

'Yeah,' Jimmy said. 'I suppose I was struck by how we seemed just as happy as one another. Or maybe . . . maybe he was happier, even. And I thought, Fuck, why did I work so hard at school? Why am I studying so hard for these exams on a Friday night, living in a shitty expensive flat, when I could have stayed near home and got a job and a nice little house and all the rest?'

'I know, but . . . would you have been satisfied, if you'd done that?' I asked. We'd never really had a conversation so personal, and I trod carefully, not wanting to cause offence or hurt. 'I guess we can't know what we don't know. But I don't think I would have, personally. I like London. I like being here. I mean, Professor Whitley . . . the guy's a legend, isn't he? Working with people like him, you don't get that in the village.'

'Maybe,' he said, hesitant. 'But, hey, you get a pint for less than three quid, at least.'

We said goodbye at the corner of my street, making plans to study together in the coming days. When I got home, midnight had just gone. I went to get myself some water from the kitchen, making sure to walk quietly, so as not to wake the others. On my way up the stairs, I noticed their bedroom doors were open and that they had gone out again.

In bed, feeling restless, I pictured Jimmy in the image he had described. A home in the village, getting into his car for an unspecified job in the neighbouring town, perhaps with a wife and kid waving to him from the door. What was odd was that I had no problem imagining this scene for Jimmy, but when I tried to insert myself in his stead, the image in my mind vanished. Maybe there was something prescient there – for Jimmy did end up going back to the village a year or so later. We finished our third year, got our degrees and quietly he left London to make his way home.

I would see him sometimes, when I came to visit. We'd exchange pleasantries, I'd give him an update on my life and he'd tell me about working on the farm. But I sensed he had no strong desire to continue our friendship, which I could understand. Likely, I had become to him nothing but a bitter reminder of what could have been. And if I'm to be completely frank, when he left a part of me felt relief, swiftly swallowed by guilt. I wasn't able to put it into words back then, but I think it had to do with that irritability I had felt on my first trip back to the village, more than a year before. That urge I had in London, to work out who I was without any anchors, without anyone who reminded me of home. I wanted to be in a place empty of anyone able to show me my reflection, so that I could forge it myself.

8

The Ormond Scholarship ended up going to Lea Mann and me, a little after we started dating in our third year. I look back at that time fondly, though I think we knew early on that our relationship was not meant to last. It was founded more on practical convenience than anything else: we were in the same department, lived near one another in Kentish Town, and had mutual friends. We got together in the second term, after a group of us went out for a drink following a late night at the library. She'd had her hair cut the week before, her dark blonde locks now falling on her shoulders, and I told her it suited her. 'I didn't know you were the kind of guy who noticed when girls got haircuts,' she said, pleased. She invited me back to hers, and the next day asked if I wanted to see the Louise Bourgeois exhibition at the Tate. We spent the whole day together, having lunch in Borough Market, strolling along the South Bank in the evening, observing the book stalls and the people mudlarking on the Thames. Afterwards I went to hers again, and then we were together.

I already knew from our seminars that Lea was an idealist. She was studying engineering to create a better world: using maths and science to shape its structures in a way that benefitted nature and us. It was hard for her to understand how anyone could be taking these classes for any other reason. A month or two into our relationship, I went with her to the careers fair. I didn't really see the point in going as we already knew we were going on to postgraduate studies in the autumn.

It was an incredibly hot day, and the room had large windows that amplified the heat. It felt sizzling, and was overcrowded with students riffling through various stands, NGOs and law firms, banks and large corporations. Lea went to the Greenpeace stand, and I was left to my own devices. I walked around the room absently. I passed the Royal Navy stand and glanced at one of the brochures, not really paying attention, until the officer there approached me. 'Ever considered joining the Navy, son?' Now that I think about it, I doubt he could have been much older than me: 'son' was an odd choice.

I'd wondered about a career in the armed forces, if only in passing. I had two cousins in the army, who'd come visit the village when I was a child, in the summer. They had medals and scars and stories of the Gulf War that I couldn't, at the time, fully comprehend. What has stayed with me is how they looked when holding the porcelain teacups and biscuits my mother had prepared, giant and strong and out of place, and the way my father watched them as they told their stories: the same way that the audience had been transfixed by Masuda on *Late Night*, with awe and esteem.

The officer asked me what I was studying and when I told him he smiled in approval. He dived into his speech about the various roles they offered, the career paths and the benefits. I was intrigued, if only because I'd never talked to a naval officer before. I was on the verge of asking him about deployment when I felt a tug on my sleeve.

'What are you doing?' Lea said. 'Come on, I want to show you something.' I thanked the officer, and as she pulled me away, I grabbed a brochure and shoved it into my pocket.

'Why were you talking to him?' she said. 'You can't seriously be interested in that.'

'I was just curious,' I said. 'There's no harm in asking some questions.'

I should say that we were then in the midst of the Iraq War. Military decisions were at the peak of public mistrust. 'We're the top students in our year, you and I,' Lea told me, later that evening. She was sitting cross-legged on my bed, wearing an old T-shirt of mine. 'There's so much you can achieve. There're so many good things you'll be able to do. Please don't waste it by going into Blair's moronic war machine.'

'I didn't say I would. I mean, am I not allowed to consider any other options than your holy path towards world preservation?'

'Ha-ha. Make fun of me all you want. At least I have morals. Don't you feel a sense of responsibility? A sense of duty to use our skills for good?'

'You're acting as if the whole world is black and white,' I said. 'It doesn't work like that. There's no straight line that divides the universe between good and evil, Lea.'

'I know that. I'm not an idiot. But whatever you do in the Navy, you'll be a pawn. You might travel the world and do some cool missions, yes. And you'll do some good deeds too, no doubt. Rescues and minesweeping and all that. But there will be wars, like there are now. And wars you might not believe in and, yes, that might be evil, and yet you'll have to fight in them.'

She got up, went to the mirror and tied her hair into a bun, revealing her nape. Her curves were visible through my T-shirt. She got into bed and I sat next to her, caressing her legs. Our words soothed, coming to a truce, and I watched her breathing soften as she fell asleep.

Though I dismissed what she had said, over the years I've found myself revisiting Lea's words. For my master's thesis,

I wrote about nuclear reactors: a device to house and control nuclear fission, in which atoms split and release energy, which could then be used to power engines. Professor Whitley was one of the leaders in the field, and nuclear science was experiencing a boom in research, with many funding opportunities. Was I aware that the technology was then used almost exclusively by the military? Yes. Did I recognise that my research was, hence, research into how best to fuel war vehicles? Yes and no.

Back then I was an idealist too, though not in the same sense as Lea. Rather, I believed that all scientific and technological progress was, in essence, good. I saw the world as a field of possibilities waiting to be sown, and I thought that what fertilised, what actualised those possibilities was tangible human progress, not morals and principles. And I believed that any harm that arose from said progress was a regrettable, but unavoidable, by-product. I cannot be certain that this is true, but that's not to say I regret my research. In a matter of years, nuclear energy would power not just military vehicles but almost all spacecraft – and my knowledge in the field gave me an unquestionable advantage.

When I did join the Navy as a submariner, straight after my master's, I didn't join entirely of my own volition. It was 2008 and we were in the midst of the biggest financial crisis in almost a century. Even the largest tech companies, which a year before would have come knocking at our department's door, had frozen their recruitment programmes. What was I supposed to do? I knew the Navy would provide me with a secure position and engineering chartership. I knew it would give me the opportunity to work on a running nuclear reactor, which powered submarines, and that I would have the chance to travel the world and expand my horizons.

After uni, Lea went on to work for an organisation that provided access to clean water. I used to see her name come up in scientific journals, and I was always glad to know she was doing well. Sometimes, when I've done my tasks for the day and *Talos* is quiet, I try to imagine my life had I followed her path. But then I look out of the viewing port. I see the crescent moon and the faint shimmers of Venus and Mars. I see the deepest dark that surrounds us infinitely, awash with stars and the misty hues of nebulas, their rich purples, their vibrant reds. I see the Milky Way in all its glory, untainted by city lights, and the sun rising over Earth's atmosphere. I see them all, those celestial lights, and I know that no other path would have shown them to me.

PHOENIX MISSION
Commander Oliver Ines's Personal Log

Talos, Day 1538. Great Red Spot fully visible now.

Atmosphere on board a bit dull. It takes only one of us to be a tad downbeat for the rest to follow, as if low moods are contagious. I try to remain alert to any of my crew's change in behaviour, like Shane's bout of depression earlier in the year.

I entered the pilot deck in the morning to check on Dom. I saw that he was reading his Bible again.

'Hey,' I said.

He jumped. 'Oh, hey, Ollie. You scared me.'

'Sorry,' I said. I moved closer to him, and pointed at his book. 'What passage are you reading?'

'Psalms,' he said. He read a few verses.

'O Lord, our Lord, how majestic is your name in all the earth! You have set your glory above the heavens ...

When I look at your heavens, the work of your fingers, the Moon and the stars, which you have set in place,

what is man that you are mindful of him, and the son of man that you care for him? ...'

He considered the page for a little while.

'What does that mean, to you?' I asked gently.

He pondered the question. 'Look at all this,' he said, pointing around the cockpit, to the large window, from which you could see the galaxy. 'And look at us. If God created all those immense entities — the planets, the universe, everything ... if He had the power to create that, and then He chose to create us — small, frail, beings. Why would He waste His power on us? And more than that, why would He give us the keys to His creations? The intellect to twist His elements, all of His designs, into machines that give us dominion over His universe?'

'Maybe,' I said, 'he would have made us just smart enough to be able to appreciate His work in all its glory, but weak enough so that we would remain fearful of Him. So that we wouldn't destroy what He had created.'

'Maybe,' he said, his brows furrowed. 'You're not religious, are you?'

'I'm not,' I said, in an apologetic tone. 'Growing up, there was a church in my village. Almost everyone went on Sundays. It wasn't only about religion. It was something to do, you know? A social gathering. There wasn't much else going on. But, my parents and I, we never went. I think some neighbours weren't pleased about it. But my dad wouldn't budge. Even when I'd beg to go because all the other kids did. He was - is - a very rational man. He just couldn't play along with something that couldn't be proven.'

'Ah,' Dom said. 'I know where you got that from, then. Your rationality, I mean.'

'I guess I am a bit like that, aren't I?' I said.

Dom chuckled again. 'Yeah, but you're a dreamer too. We all are, the four of us, aren't we? Otherwise we wouldn't be here. You have to be a bit mad, to do what we did.' He leaned towards the cockpit, one hand holding on to his Bible. 'We were the opposite, you and I,' he continued. 'I was in the choir for my local church in St Louis, did you know that? "Little Dominic, he's got the voice of an angel," people used to say. But then ... I don't know. In the Air Force, in Iraq ...' He shook his head. He gave his Bible a tap. 'I couldn't see any holiness in it. I couldn't see any signs of God.'

'And now?' I said, after a short time had passed.

He stared out the window, and I followed suit, my left hand clinging to the handrail. 'Do I think that God created this universe in six days? No. But do I think ... that it's a miracle we're here? The Big Bang, oxygen, water, the position of the sun ... All of these things, billions of them, that had to be exactly right, for humanity to come into existence. And, sure, you can think about it just in terms of science. But me – and I've given this question a lot of time in the past couple of years, on this deck right here ... I choose to believe that it's a divine act.' He turned to face me, smiling. 'I choose to believe that it is the work of God.'

I returned his smile.

'But, hey, keep this chat between us, won't ya?' he said, before turning his attention back to the deck.

I didn't need to ask why he said that. There's a tendency on board to turn everything into banter: a movie you like, a hobby you've developed on board, your beliefs ... Nothing is really safe from being turned into the butt of a joke, except families and homesickness. In any case, I'm glad I checked on Dom. It's easy to forget sometimes, when we're each busy with our tasks, how well we get on, the four of us. And

I have to say, when he told me that this journey had deepened his faith, I was almost relieved. It would have been quite dire to learn it had had the opposite effect.

9

I haven't given the Ormond Scholarship much thought over the years. Why should I have? I felt – I still feel – like I'd worked hard enough to be deserving of it. I'm not sure why it's been on my mind lately. When I have a minute to myself on *Talos*, usually after dinner, I try to read my book but my mind will wander to that time in my life. I'll picture the fallen leaves on the ground, their autumnal shades, guiding us to the fountain in a straight walk. I'll feel the sharp wind on my face and the coffee cup hot in my hands, and then I'll picture Jimmy's crestfallen expression, a plea for help, and I feel my mind trying to brush the image away.

It was at the start of our final undergraduate year, in 2006, a few months before Lea Mann and I got together. Jimmy had spent his summer helping his parents at the farm, whereas I'd stayed in London for most of it. It was one of the only times in the year when all my flatmates were away and, even if it was falling apart, having the flat to myself felt like a luxurious treat. I gave it a thorough clean, scrubbing away the mould and limescale in the shower, the oil stains and grease that had clung to the kitchen stove. I got rid of the old mouse traps that hadn't worked and Ben's rotten tomatoes on his fridge shelf. Once I was done hoovering, the whole place felt light and new.

I worked part-time at a bookshop in Kentish Town, mostly on weekdays when it was quiet, so that I could spend a good part of the day reading or browsing the shelves. I read a lot of Russian novels that summer, either at the shop or on the balcony off our kitchen. It had a foldable chair, a side table and a herb garden that smelled of rosemary, hanging from the railing.

Jimmy suggested we go for a walk in Regent's Park. It had rained the night before and the ground was covered with slick leaves, so we walked carefully. We bought coffee from the outdoor café. 'How did you do in your exams?' Jimmy asked. I told him I'd done pretty well, all firsts except for one module in which I'd got a high 2:1. I asked him how he'd done, and I gathered we were, once again, neck and neck.

'You're still thinking about doing a master's?' he asked, as we left the café.

'Yeah,' I said. 'I'm working on my application, actually. You?'

'I think so,' he said. He paused, finding his words. I removed the lid from my coffee, blowing on it to cool it.

'Remember that chat we had in the spring, at the Goldhawk?' Jimmy continued. 'When I told you about Daniel Wilson?'

'I do,' I said. 'Did you see him again?'

'No, no,' he said. 'I was at the farm most of the time. But I just . . . I think about this stuff, sometimes.'

'You mean, if you should have stayed in the village?'

'Yeah,' he said. 'Sometimes.'

We reached the big drinking fountain on Broad Walk. He gestured for us to take a seat on one of the benches nearby. There were a few tourists around, children in pushchairs, but it was mostly quiet. I don't recall how the rest of our conversation went exactly, but it was clear that Jimmy had been dwelling on the matter. He moved his coffee from one hand to the other, his expression hesitant. 'Truth is, I liked working at the farm, this summer,' he said, as if reluctant to admit it. 'Something about it felt so much more – alive? Yeah – so much more alive than what we do here. It felt more rewarding.'

'I don't know,' I said. 'I think what we do is pretty rewarding.' I thought about telling him what my dad had told me all those years ago. That engineering was about making things greater than the sum of their parts, that we were the bridge between dreams and realities, but I didn't want to sound naïve.

Would it have made a difference, if I had? I doubt it. It

seemed to me that what he really sought that day was someone to validate his feelings. That he had come to me with his mind already made up, and all he wanted from me was permission. He told me more about the farm and about his doubts, and in the end I just said, 'Listen. You've been feeling like this for a while, haven't you? I don't know . . . if you're not happy here, what's the point in persisting? You can finish this year with a good bachelor's degree, then go home, work on the farm, do whatever you want to do. And you can always change your mind, come back, you know? Imperial's not going anywhere.'

'Yeah,' he said, contemplating what I'd said. 'You might be right.' He drank his coffee, and afterwards a smile appeared on his face. 'Thanks, Ollie. I'm glad we could talk.'

10

A year after that walk, when I began my master's – after I'd received the scholarship, after Lea and I had dated and Jimmy had left London – I went to Professor Whitley's office to ask him if he would supervise my thesis. I took a cautious step into his office, straightening my jacket and my posture, as he stayed in his chair.

'Congratulations, Oliver,' he said, with a coolness I was not expecting.

'Thank you,' I said. 'I couldn't have done it without all your advice.'

He gave a polite nod. He stood up and went to face his window. It gave a view of an office building that blocked the sunlight, so that the room remained dark throughout the day. His cluttered desk occupied most of the space. Everywhere you laid your eyes there were piles of old textbooks and papers, and bookshelves packed with rows of identical binders lined the walls. By his desk, framed, hung various prestigious accreditations.

He continued, still facing away. 'I heard James Lovett

decided not to apply. That he decided to go home, in the end.'

'He did,' I said. 'He's helping his parents on their farm now, I believe.'

'A shame,' he said. 'He was a very promising student. I wish someone could have given him more encouragement.'

'Yes,' I said, unnerved. 'It's a shame. But he seemed set on his decision.'

'I'm sure he was.' He turned towards me. His figure was fully shaded, and I couldn't quite read his expression. 'He told me you two spoke about it.'

'I . . . Yes, we did,' I said. 'Only briefly, though. I think he was pretty set by the time we did.'

'I see,' he said, observing me closely. 'Well, I suppose it worked out. After all, we couldn't have given the scholarship to both of you.'

When I've replayed the exchange in my mind, I cannot mistake the note of accusation in his tone.

'Couldn't you, sir?' I said. 'I thought it was given to two students in the department.'

'That's true,' he said. 'But the odds that the committee would have given it to you two, two candidates with such similar profiles . . . well, I don't think that was likely, in all honesty. No, Lea Mann was always going to be the other recipient. And a very deserving young woman, I must say. She edged you both in finals.'

'Well, I certainly didn't know all that,' I said, hot under my jacket.

'No, no, of course,' he added quickly. 'You had no way of knowing.'

Slowly, he sat down again. I kept my eyes trained on the piles of books on the floor. 'Do you know what you wish to do, after next year?' he asked.

'I'm not sure yet,' I said, uncertain as to where the conversation was going. 'Not many places are recruiting, right now. But I was thinking of perhaps joining the Navy. As a submariner.'

He made a noise that suggested he was impressed. 'I know an engineer back in Cambridge who began his career like that. It's tough,' he said. 'Months at a time beneath the ocean. No contact at all with the outside world.'

'Yes,' I said. 'But they'll offer the best engineering opportunities. And I think . . . well, it must be quite a unique experience, right?'

'Just because a path is unique,' he said, matter-of-factly, 'doesn't mean it's worth pursuing.'

'No, no,' I said. 'Of course. I know that.' I explained my reasoning in more detail, the nuclear reactor, the chartership. He listened patiently, leant back in his chair, his right hand on his chin. When I was done he took a moment before speaking.

'Listen, Oliver,' he said with a new intensity, sliding forward in his chair. 'I've seen lots of students come and go over the years. Some who might not show much promise at first, but end up surprising me. And many who I think will go far, but who come up short of those expectations. Students who give up on their ambitions, and seek a different path, whatever it might be. And I've concluded that what really distinguishes the former from the latter is ruthlessness.'

His words echoed in the room. I felt something twisting in my stomach.

'Ruthlessness, sir?' I asked.

'Yes. I don't mean cruelty, or anything like that. No, what I mean is that great ambitions, *unique* achievements, as you called them, often come hand in hand with the – rather regrettable – ability to go forward in life, no matter the cost.'

With relief I saw his face relax – as if he had offered nothing more than stern advice.

'And so, since we'll be working closely this year, Oliver, I'll tell you this. You belong to the first class of students. You didn't stand out much to me in your first year, but you've turned out to be quite an impressive young man. I have no doubt you'll go very far, if you desire to do so.'

'Thank you,' I said, unsure how to feel about those remarks. 'That's very good to hear.'

'Yes,' he said. 'And I can already see with the Navy that you're embarking on a path in which you'll have to sacrifice many things. Your family, your home, your friends . . . They can hold a person back, like with our friend James. They'll have to fall secondary to your ambitions.' I thought about Hatsuo Masuda on *Late Night* in his JAXA suit, smiling gently. *It's just part of the job.* 'You'll have to be single-minded, in what you prioritise in your life.'

Without waiting for a response, Professor Whitley turned his attention to his desk, shuffling stacks of paper around, signalling that our conversation was coming to a close. And as I approached the door, glad of escape, it was his parting words that left the sharpest impression on me. 'But then again,' he said curtly, picking up a pen, 'I have a feeling that won't be too much of a problem for you. Have a good beginning of term, Oliver. I'll see you next month for our first meeting.'

11

It would be too easy for me to say that I regret discouraging Jimmy from applying for the scholarship. What if he had received it over me? No doubt my life would have taken a much different turn. For one, I wouldn't have met Shane.

It was at the start of term one. Shane and I were both interested in nuclear reactors so Professor Whitley put us in touch. Perhaps out of arrogance I wasn't pleased to have been paired with an undergraduate. I was already drowning in work on my thesis: I didn't want to spend time mentoring a younger student. But Professor Whitley assured me he was a 'bright young thing' and that it would be beneficial for both of us.

We met at the library café on campus. It was one of those days of the year on which summer lingered, and students were making the most of it, sitting all over the Queen's Lawn, taking in the sun. I waited in front of the café in the shade, conscious of perspiring through my white shirt. Shane arrived ten minutes late, muttering something about his alarm not going off. He was taller than me by about an inch, with dark-red messy hair, as if he'd just got out of bed. His slouched demeanour made him seem a relaxed, mellow character, but as soon as you began talking to him properly you could see how alert and quick-witted he was. It's no wonder that he became a pilot. That mix of cool-headed calm and laser focus made him perfect for the job.

I suggested we go inside as it would be quieter and he agreed grudgingly, gazing wistfully at the students lounging in the heat. I came prepared with a list of papers and books I believed might help him in his research. It'd taken me the whole evening to put it together. I'd added a line underneath each entry, explaining the main idea behind the paper. When I handed the list to him, a touch proudly perhaps, he merely glanced at it before shoving it into his backpack. 'Thanks,' he said. 'I think I'm all set for now.'

'Okay,' I said. 'Well, I'd have a read either way, if I were you. The Lewis paper, especially – I really got a lot out of that one—'

'Hey, can I ask you something?' he interrupted.
'Yes?'
'What's up with Professor Whitley's ties?'
'Oh, well, I don't know. I guess he likes to wear extravagant ones. For fun.'
'No,' he said. 'That's not it. I feel like he's using them as a

distraction. Maybe from his balding head. Have you noticed? He should just wear a hat. That's what my brother does.'

'I haven't been paying attention to his head that much.'

'How could you not?' he said. 'It's so shiny.'

I left the café with a strong dislike for Shane. When I asked him about our first encounter years later, he went red in the face. 'I wondered if you were ever going to bring that up,' he said. 'Poor old Professor Whitley.' He apologised for, as he called it, his 'dickhead behaviour'. 'I was just nervous,' he said, as we were having lunch in the cafeteria.

'Why?' I asked.

'I mean, you were one of the rock stars of the department. You were already getting published in major journals! I didn't want you to think I was lame.'

We met again when term was in full swing, students and teachers hurrying to classes across campus. Though he still acted with a nonchalance that irked me, as we caught up I understood that he'd studied all the readings I'd suggested. I saw, as Professor Whitley had spotted, that he was indeed a 'bright young thing'. We talked about Mark Massey. NovaTech had recently announced plans for the HEPHA mission, in collaboration with the ESA – the European Space Agency – due to launch in 2016. Its aim was to send four astronauts to Mars, headed once more by Masuda, who had only just returned from that same planet on the EROS mission, his triumphant face headlining every newspaper in the world.

The HEPHA spacecraft, *Pegasus*, was to be equipped with a nuclear propulsion system twice as efficient as the chemical model used at the time. Heat from the nuclear reactor would be transferred into a liquid fuel, then turned into gas, which would provide thrust. The mission would take 700 days, half the time of the EROS mission.

We all assumed that Massey was mad: no engine would be able to sustain the extreme heat required for the propulsion system to work at that scale. Nuclear reactors had been used to power small spacecraft, yes, some probes and the like – but never on a craft big enough to carry humans, let alone four.

'Can you imagine?' I said. 'If his model works. Complete game-changer.'

'It won't,' Shane said. 'Not on his timeline. The science isn't there yet. I bet it's a PR stunt, more than anything else.'

'I don't know. The first tests are promising . . .'

'Ollie, if it works, I promise you, I'll give you a hundred quid. Two hundred, even.'

'Okay. You've got a deal.'

As the end of the year neared, Shane invited me to his Christmas party. It was an annual and great affair that he hosted with his flatmates, Matteo, Liv and Jade. The gossipy echoes of last year's event had reached even me. 'Come along,' he said. 'Almost all the department will be there.'

I didn't like parties much. More often than not I would find myself half-trapped in a conversation, lukewarm beer or wine in hand and wishing to be at home, the next day's hangover never quite worth it. They gave me the impression of being in a fishbowl, in view of everyone, like in Professor Whitley's seminars. I was about to decline with the excuse of a looming deadline, when I saw Shane's insistent look: it seemed to matter to him that I come. I told him I'd drop by.

They lived in an old church conversion on Greenland Road, with high arched ceilings and a damp problem. By the time I arrived, the house teemed with students. 'Ollie!' Liv said, as she hugged me and took my fleece. 'Shane's told us all about you. He's in the kitchen.' I thanked her and elbowed my way to the kitchen, dropping off my pack of Red Stripe in the fridge, taking one out. The room smelt of cigarettes and sweat. Shane was there, chatting to a girl. He didn't take any notice of me. Not wanting to interrupt, I simply gave him a nod and made my way to the living room.

I couldn't recognise anyone I knew. I scanned the room for a discreet corner to stand, and to give my hands something to do I began drinking my beer. After searching the room again, I spotted two postgraduates smoking on the sofa, waving at me.

'Oliver Ines!' one said, as I approached. I didn't know his name. 'So kind of you to join us.'

The other smirked. 'We didn't think you came to this sort of thing,' she said.

'What do you mean?'

'Well, you're Professor Whitley's favourite. Top of the class and all that. We thought maybe you considered us beneath you.' They laughed, and I followed suit.

'Not at all,' I said. 'Afraid I don't get invited to these much. Next time, give me a shout.' I gave them a polite smile and made small-talk, and under the pretence of getting another drink I left quickly after.

In the *Time* article, there was a quote from a fellow postgraduate, who remained anonymous, that stung me: 'I don't think any of us were really shocked when he joined the mission. We always thought he was a little strange – always civil, but not very interested in other human beings, if that makes sense. He was a loner, definitely. We rarely saw him outside campus.' I've always wondered if that quote came from one of those two at the party. I don't think it was a particularly fair thing to say. I wasn't the most talkative or outgoing person, true, but I don't think I was ever rude, or anything other than polite and friendly. That year, especially, had left me with almost no time to socialise: I had a thesis to write, on top of applying to the Navy. But students seemed to mistake my quiet manner for aloofness.

I went to the bathroom. In the mirror I saw that my whole face was crimson. Even my eyes had been stung red by the smoke. As part of the Navy application I'd had to start going to the gym, but in my reflection I could see no difference in my appearance, lanky and slim. I looked at my watch. I'd been at the party for half an hour. I had to stay for at least an hour, I told myself. Someone knocked on the door and, reluctantly, I left the bathroom.

In the kitchen, Shane was now snogging the girl. I'd been wrong in assuming it was important for him that I come, and reprimanded myself for having thought so. In the living room, some students were dancing and others hung out of the windows, cigarettes in their hands. The noise of faraway ambulances and drunken passers-by floated up to us. The two postgraduates were doing coke on the dining table.

Finally, another half an hour had ticked by. I went to say a quick goodbye to Shane. 'You're going already?' he said. 'Alright, I'll see you in the new year, yeah?' He gave me a quick hug and turned back towards the girl. I went into his bedroom and rifled through the pile of scarves and bags, woollen coats and parkas on his bed until I found my fleece smothered at the bottom, all crumpled.

Just as I grabbed it, trying to smooth it out, I heard a voice coming from the door.

'Ollie?'

I looked up, startled, and there she was. She wore dark eyeliner, her hair was shorter, with its tips dyed electric blue, but I recognised her instantly. 'Philly?' I said.

She reached for a hug. 'It's so great to see you,' she said, as dazed as I was. We could barely hear each other over the music and had to lean into one another. 'What are you doing here?'

'I'm a friend of Shane,' I said. 'We're in the same department. You?'

'Friend of Jade. We're doing biology at UCL.' She smiled. 'Where to begin, right? It's been what – eleven, twelve years? We need to have a proper catch-up.' I noticed that she was not alone. Behind her was a tall, good-looking man, eyeing me with curiosity. She followed my gaze. 'Oh, this is Josh by the way! Josh, this is Ollie. He's the guy I told you about, remember? From my aunt's village.'

'Oh, yeah!' he said. 'It's nice to meet you.'

'Likewise,' I said, shaking his hand. He had on a large grin, which made me wonder what Philly had told him about me. I turned to face her, and I saw how radiant she was. It was as if all of the features she had had as a girl – the curve of her nose, her round lips, her large, round eyes – had been refined into their purest forms. I pictured my crimson face from the bathroom mirror, and I became self-conscious. The noises and the crush of people, the smell of cigarettes and sweat, Josh's grin and the uncanniness of the situation overwhelmed me. I had a strong urge to leave.

'Have you just arrived?' Philly said, pointing at my fleece.

'I was on my way out, actually.'

'Oh,' she said. 'That's a shame. Won't you stay for one more drink?'

'I wish, but I've got a paper due in a couple of days,' I said, though that wasn't exactly true: I'd already handed it in. 'Need to go to the library first thing tomorrow. But it'd be nice to catch up soon.'

'Yes, please! Add me on Facebook,' she said. 'My name is Dean. Philly Dean.'

PHOENIX MISSION
Commander Oliver Ines's Personal Log

Talos, Day 1550. Good atmosphere on board. Very slowly, we edge closer to Europa.

An interesting day. We were all done with our tasks and relaxing in our own ways. Dom was in the control deck, Shane watching some comedy series, Lucia reading a book, and I was playing chess with A-T (I've had to increase his difficulty level to 7, which pleased me). The stillness was interrupted here and there with Shane's loud laugh, but I didn't mind: it was pleasant to feel some life on board.

After about an hour of this, Dom appeared. 'Hey, Ollie. Can you come, please?'

I followed him to the control deck.

'I was surveying our trajectory. I noticed the autopilot rerouted us slightly, yesterday. That happens sometimes, to avoid some debris or micrometeorite or anything that wasn't picked up before we left. Nothing to worry about, and it won't make much of a difference to our timeline. But I was trying to see what we're avoiding, and ... well, look.'

He pointed at the screen, at a very blurry, pixellated photo that A-T had taken of the 'unidentified object', as it said underneath.

'That's man-made, isn't it?' I asked. 'Not a meteorite.'

'Yep,' he said. 'It's hundreds of thousands of miles away, so we don't have a clear visual. But, see the dimensions, here? That's a spacecraft. It's missing some bits. But it was a large one, that's for sure. Large enough to carry humans.'

We both observed the photo again, trying to make sense of it. But as much as we tried, it wasn't clear enough for us to establish what model it could be.

'So you're saying it's ... wreckage?'

'Looks like it. But it's odd. There hasn't been an accident since—'

'HEPHA,' I interrupted. '*Pegasus*. Of this size, at least.'

'Right,' he said. 'Not since we left, anyway.'

We stayed quiet, mesmerised by the remains of the spacecraft.

'Should we tell the others?' he asked.

'Yes,' I said. 'Do you think you could get us closer?'

'To the wreckage? I mean, the autopilot's guiding us away from it. I suppose I could override it, bring us a bit closer, see if we can spot any clues on the model and things like that ... but, Ollie, it's risky.'

'I know,' I said. 'But isn't that why we're here? Not just for Europa, but to explore. To uncover mysteries of the universe.'

He laughed nervously. He moved his hand behind his neck, in a gesture that seemed to indicate discomfort.

'You're a clever one, aren't you?'

'Not really,' I said. 'Merely curious. What's your risk assessment?'

'Not that high. Even if we change our trajectory by point one, that should get us close enough to have a decent view of it.' He paused, examining the screen. 'Look, Ollie, I want to as well. Feels like Fate, doesn't it? That we'd see this. But we've got to talk to the others before we make a call.'

'Alright,' I said. 'I'll set up a meeting for first thing tomorrow.'

We exchanged a few more words, and then I left him to it and arranged the meeting. I have to say, this 'unidentified object' has got me feeling an eagerness I haven't experienced for a while. Perhaps a bit of novelty is just what the crew needs to keep us all going.

PART II

12

Sometimes, when I'm doing maintenance on *Talos*, I'll think of *Valiant*. They were similar in a lot of ways: confined spaces in hostile environments, cut off from the outside world. Despite the different laws of physics, the work on *Valiant* was not so different – and a specific movement or tool is enough to unlock memories I thought I'd lost. Only last week I conducted a minor repair on *Talos*'s hatch that leads to the storage lockers. I applied lubricant to the door's hinges, wiping off the excess with a tissue, and I was brought back to my younger self, doing the same swift movement on *Valiant* twenty years or so ago.

HMS *Valiant* was a ballistic submarine, carrying the UK's nuclear deterrent and about 130 seamen. A good part of my work there remains classified. Secret missions, new technologies – things I've convinced myself didn't occur, and as a result my recollections of them are dreamlike, shrouded and blurred. Which is why they came to me on *Talos* as a welcome surprise.

My first time at sea was in the winter of 2011. I was twenty-five, finished with my training in Dartmouth and freshly made a sub-lieutenant. It was a short mission, two months, and to this day I don't know where we were posted. I spent my mornings at the rear of the boat helping with engine work: checks on the reactor, maintenance on the machines and the ventilation systems. The first half of the boat lodged the control, the sound rooms and our living quarters, where I spent the rest of my day. Ravi, also an officer – we shared a room back at our base in Faslane – sometimes lent me his computer. 'I've filled it with all the Arnie movies,' he told me on our first day.

'Who's Arnie?' I said.

His eyes went wide. 'Schwarzenegger,' he said. 'Arnold Schwarzenegger. Mate, please tell me you know who that is.'

'Course I do,' I said. 'I just didn't know he went by Arnie.'

'Well,' he said, 'they're all there. *Terminator*, *Conan*, *Predator*. Even *Twins*. You've seen that one? People forget, but he's a great comedic actor as well.'

I nodded, though I didn't really know what he was talking about (I hadn't seen *Twins*).

'Oh,' he said, pointing at a little folder on his desktop. He gave me a mischievous grin. 'And this is, you know, *other* kinds of movies.' He winked at me. 'Don't open it in public, please.'

Besides those chats with Ravi, I didn't socialise very much during those first weeks on board. The morning work was tiring, and I wasn't yet used to the intensity of life on a submarine. It was almost impossible to have time on your own, and to avoid the awareness that you were only a leak or mishap away from a horrible death. Yet there was also an odd sense of tranquillity that arose from being so remote, thousands of feet beneath the ocean's surface. We slept in racks with curtains for privacy, and I would write my diary there and read. I read more than I ever had in my life, all the Zolas and the Dostoyevskys, the books I'd been meaning to read for years. Sometimes I liked to imagine that I was some kind of monk, perhaps in the Middle Ages or the Renaissance, living deep in foggy mountains somewhere with my fellows, *Valiant* the monastery we had to maintain, Captain Lowes our abbot.

In those first few weeks, I was very much in my own world. But it didn't take long for me to realise it wouldn't do. As in my university days, I felt adrift from my colleagues. A mild sense of disapproval followed me wherever I went. I would feel the discreet looks they threw at one another as I entered the officers' mess, hear the sneer in their tone as they asked me what I'd been up to that afternoon. But perhaps I was imagining all of this. I hadn't forgotten the remarks of those two postgraduates: 'We thought you considered us beneath you.'

Whether real or not, I didn't want any creeping differences to evolve into something more. The last thing *Valiant* needed was more tension: being in a submarine, carrying a dozen nuclear missiles, was enough. I spent the morning pondering how best to break the ice. In the end, I settled on the simplest approach. I went about my work, and once I had finished my shift, I washed my hands and went into the mess. It was a room where we could relax, eat and socialise, consisting of three or four wooden tables and chairs, some board and card games, a small kitchen unit, a TV and a PlayStation.

Ravi, Laurie, Oscar and a couple of other young officers were there, about to play a game of Shithead. Ravi shuffled the cards. We exchanged hellos as I entered and made my way to the kitchen unit. 'Anyone want a tea?' I asked.

I made everyone's drinks, and once I'd brought the mugs to the table I lingered in the room, studying the collection of video games neatly piled by the TV.

Ravi took notice of me. 'Would you like to join us?' he said.

'Yes, please,' I said. 'If it's no trouble.'

I turned out to be good at Shithead. 'Beginner's luck,' Ravi said, after I'd won, and then we played FIFA. That was enough, really, to get rid of the awkwardness I'd felt, and from then on the trip was plain sailing.

Not long after that first mission, I saw Shane in London. We were both on leave for the summer and we met at a pub near King's Cross. He'd just got his wings in the RAF and I bought the first round to celebrate. He told me stories of nightly escapades with his crew, when travelling and off duty. They would have pints and whisky and tequila, your glass magically always filled, until someone was sick or got kicked out. He told me about his mate who, on a trip to a base in Wales, was banned from the local pub because he had relieved himself all over the wooden bar, leaving it soaked and reeking.

I don't think we were quite as bad on *Valiant* – though that's not to say we were immune to laddish behaviour. I remember one time – it must have been my second or third mission – I was going to bed with a book in my hand. 'What are you reading?' a junior officer, who had the bunk across from mine, asked. I showed him the cover of *Madame Bovary*. It had a painting of a woman on it, wearing a navy dress and a jewelled updo, half-lounging on a sofa. He grabbed the book from me, and skimmed the blurb. I believe his exact words were, 'You are a fucking woofter, Ines.' The others in the dorm sniggered.

For the rest of the trip they wouldn't invite me when they played FIFA, saying I wouldn't be interested, that I was too busy reading mushy French books and getting my nails done. From then on, I was careful what book I brought with me. Not because I cared what they thought of me, not exactly – it was more that I wanted to be left alone. But I don't think the bantering was ever ill-intentioned: more likely, it came from a place of boredom and stress.

When we'd almost finished our drinks, I suggested another round, but Shane refused. 'Gotta go, I'm afraid. Meeting Liv for dinner.' He downed the rest of his glass and put on his rucksack. 'How about you? You seeing anyone else while you're here?'

'Not really,' I said. 'I'm taking the train home tonight. Haven't seen my parents since last year.'

'Well, I'm glad you're doing well. Looks like the Navy's been good for you.' And despite not knowing exactly what he meant – maybe my stance had become more relaxed, or I'd joked a bit more – I was glad he'd noticed what I'd suspected: that my first trip on *Valiant* had changed me for the better.

―――

On the train home that same evening, I checked Facebook. I had a new message from Philly.

> Ollie! Are you back on land? How was the sea? Tell me all about it, please. Things are good here, busy with studying

and the never-ending cycle of deadlines. Josh and I spent May in the Tabernas desert in Spain. It's amazing – filled with all kinds of plants that've beaten the odds to thrive in really arid conditions. Though I'm sure you'd know a thing or two about that, living in a submarine. Let me know when you're in London, we need to catch up. xx

I didn't answer straight away. I wanted to sober up before I did. My carriage was almost empty, apart from a group of loud students at the other end. Outside the window, it was getting dark. The city lights gave way to fields, and I dozed.

Ever since Shane's party, Philly and I had kept in touch. She was still at UCL, doing a PhD in biology.

'Can you believe I'm actually studying insects?' she told me, not too long after the party. We were having lunch on the Portico steps of UCL. 'I haven't changed at all, have I?'

'Not at all,' I said. 'It's nice, though. You've stayed true to yourself.'

She really had: her curiosity, her honesty, that feeling she gave of being always entirely herself around you, which made you want to be the same: it had all remained.

'It's funny,' she continued. 'When I saw you at Shane's, I was afraid we'd have absolutely nothing to say to each other. We were what, nine, when we met? And it's not like we'd even spent that much time together. What were the odds we'd get on as grown-ups?'

'I don't know,' I said. 'I mean, you get on with everyone, to be fair. For me, the odds were probably a little lower.'

'That's not true,' she said. 'You're just more guarded than me. You practically ran away from me at that party.'

'Sorry,' I said. 'I really couldn't listen to any more Lil Wayne.'

'Very funny.' She laughed. 'But really, why did you?'

'I'm not sure. I think I panicked. I don't think I was entirely convinced you were real. I thought maybe you were an imaginary friend I'd made up when I was a kid.'

'I'll take that as a compliment,' she said, after a pause. 'Like I was the most perfect friend you could have imagined.'

On the train, the students left and the carriage became empty. Outside it was pitch-black. I read Philly's message again. *Josh and I spent May in the Tabernas desert . . .* I hadn't seen her for almost two years, not since I'd left Dartmouth, and I hadn't seen Josh since Shane's Christmas party. I clicked on his profile picture, but you couldn't really see him: he was standing in front of a mountain, from far away, arms up in a victory pose. I had absolutely no reason to dislike him, and yet I did. I assumed I was just looking out for Philly, the way good friends do. It was only years later I admitted to myself that I might have been jealous.

The landscape began to feel familiar, and the train announced my stop. For the first time in almost a year, I was back in the village. I heaved my bag from the overhead rack, and as I did I noticed that my hands were shaking lightly. Leaving the train, I imagined Philly in the Tabernas desert, crouched on its soil, magnifier in her hand, observing things that only she could see.

PHOENIX MISSION
Commander Oliver Ines's Personal Log

Talos, Day 1551. We had the meeting first thing to discuss Dom's discovery.

'Fuck yeah, let's do it,' Shane said.

Lucia was more reluctant. 'I don't know, guys. Shouldn't we stick to the mission? I mean, it's not like a lot is riding on us, or anything.'

I'd been anticipating her reaction. I began drawing on the whiteboard, outlining our trajectory. 'You see, flying closer to the wreckage, it might actually mean we reach Europa a bit sooner.' Lucia's face remained doubtful. I closed the cap on my marker. 'Plus . . .' I said, 'don't you want to know?'

'Don't I want to know what?' Lucia asked.

'What it is. If it's *Pegasus*.'

'Terrible name, I always thought,' Shane said, deadpan. I waved him off with my hand.

'Of course I do,' Lucia said. 'But, Ollie, this isn't just about what we want. We can't be playing explorers. We're in space, for God's sake. If one little thing goes wrong, it's kaboom for us. I don't think we should override the autopilot.'

'Okay,' I said. Dom and Shane now seemed rather uncomfortable, glancing at each other. I chose my words carefully, and did my best to hide my frustration. 'I hear you. We don't have to decide right away. A day won't make a difference, anyway. Why don't we all take the day and the night to think about it, and then we can decide in the morning.'

Everyone nodded, and after a short while, we went about our day. I'm writing this just before getting off to bed.

Needless to say, Lucia is outnumbered three to one: we'll go to see the wreckage. But I do hope she comes through in the morning. I certainly would prefer that, rather than taking her there against her will. We shall see tomorrow.

13

I suppose it wasn't until I joined the Navy that I truly began to understand what Masuda had meant on *Late Night*. On *Valiant*, we could receive only two emails from our families per week, of no more than sixty words each. We weren't allowed to respond for fear of giving away our location to enemy intelligence: our role was to be hidden and silent, a killer whale ready to strike at any second.

Valiant wasn't ideal for romance: who wants to date someone who's unreachable for half the year? So, apart from a couple of short-lived relationships, I was single for most of my first years in the Navy. Only my parents messaged me. Their emails were short and sweet, a line or two about how they were doing, an update on the garden and relatives. The messages forbade any content that might distress us. According to the official guidelines, the Familygram was supposed to be no more than a 'very short message of reassurance' to be sent 'to someone who has no method of returning home should something be wrong'. Of course, if there was a true emergency – a bereavement, life-threatening injury or illness – arrangements could be made. You could be dropped off at a rendezvous point, though it could take days, and would disrupt the mission and create a large fuss for the rest of the crew. Before deployment, we had to discuss with our family and superior if we wished to receive bad news while at sea and, like most men, I asked that it be withheld.

At first it wasn't a problem. I was in my mid-twenties, armed with the belief that my loved ones and I were invincible. I didn't realise that while I was away for months at a time the world stayed in motion and my parents went on living their lives – and that life went on happening to them too. I came home for Christmas 2012, after my longest mission yet: twelve weeks at sea.

The village was all dressed up, twinkly lights adorning the houses and giant baubles on the naked trees, frosted snowflakes in the Shield's windows. My father came to pick me up from the station. It had snowed all night and the road home was slippery and white so we drove slowly. His demeanour told me something was amiss: he spoke in a way that was fast and jittery, and he fired questions at me, though he'd never been much of a talker. He had stubble on his lower face, which I'd never seen.

'So, you're enjoying it, then? I know you can't tell me

much about your trip,' he said. 'But do you prefer being in Faslane or at sea?'

'It's more fun to be at sea,' I said. 'Obviously the conditions are hard. But when you're at base, you feel like you're in a state of limbo. You want to get back out there.'

'I see,' he said. 'I see. Still, must be alright, to get to travel, right?'

'Right.'

He turned on the radio, and we listened to the news.

'How about you and Mum? How've things been?'

'Oh, you know us. Same as always.'

He turned left, and there, in the distance, was my childhood home. 'That's good,' I said. 'Well, it's good to be back.'

'Yes. Good to have you back. Very good.' After some hesitation, he added, 'Actually, there's something I meant to tell you. Nothing too serious, of course. But, well, your mum – she's had a bit of a . . . a health issue. No, no, don't worry, it's okay. It's just, well, she went in for a check-up a couple of months ago because she'd felt a lump round here.' He tapped his chest. 'And they did some tests and everything and . . . well . . . you know.'

He pinched his lips. His hands were clutching the wheel tightly, as he stared into the empty road.

'What is it?' I asked, bracing for the worse. His face twisted in unease.

It didn't feel real. You'd hear about people getting ill – your parents' friends, an uncle or someone from the village. You'd see it in movies and books. The news would say that one in two people would get some type of cancer in their lifetime – but nothing can prepare you for the news that your mother has it.

'We caught it early, don't worry. She had her first round of chemo two weeks ago, and we're waiting for some results back – Dr Cosler said she should make a full recovery.'

'You should've told me,' I was about to say, but I stopped: I'd made my choice. I'd asked for bad news to be withheld while I was at sea, and it had been. I fixed my eyes on the road as well, a bitter lump forming in my throat. I thought of Masuda, then of Professor Whitley, the truth of his words hitting me all at once. Willingly I had put myself out of reach of my family. I had created a gulf that even in the worst circumstances they could not cross, and now I could see, in plain sight, the ruthlessness of my action.

'Bloody hell,' I said instead.

'Yeah,' he said, in a worn-out laugh. 'That's about right.'

Mum came out of the house as we parked, small in the door frame. Her blonde curls had thinned and her face was paler than usual. When she hugged me, I felt the hollows between her bones – and I remember my whole world shifting as I realised she was not an invincible being.

'Ollie,' she said softly, holding me. I wanted to hug her tighter, but I was afraid that if I did I would break her. 'I'm so happy to see you.' When I tried to say something in return, I found that my tongue couldn't move. My dad patted our backs, not quite sure what to do.

'Come in,' Mum said. 'It's freezing outside.'

She wrapped her arm around mine, and we went to the living room. She sat in the armchair, the flames in the fireplace bathing her in a soft and warm glow. I asked how she was feeling.

'Oh, I'm okay,' she said. 'Dr Cosler and the nurses have been really kind. And your dad's been a great help, too.' I felt a pit of guilt in my stomach. My dad brought us tea, and we sipped in silence.

'This reminds me of when I was young,' she said, 'and we'd have to cuddle up by the fire to keep warm. The cold felt different, back then. Fiercer.'

She began telling me about her childhood, which she'd never done before. About sledging with her cousins, the turnip soup her mum made, the smell spreading over the house. I see it so distinctly: Mum resting in the armchair, her eyes bright, her memories flooding into the room the whole of the Christmas break.

She told me about her summers at her grandfather's; the chilling tales of the war he would tell her, and that would keep her up at night. She described to me in detail the hand-me-downs from her sisters and brothers, which were tattered and patched by the time they reached her. 'I'd get teased so much, at school. But now it's cool, isn't it, wearing hand-me-downs? Vintage, you call it.'

Sometimes she would grow tired and doze. I'd lay a blanket across her lap, and then Dad would walk her to their room, her movements brittle. I'd stay in the sitting room, absorbing the parts of her life I hadn't known before, my picture of her becoming fuller, like a drawing being coloured in. Those memories she had told me, willing to pass them on so that they could remain on Earth eternally, ghostlike and immortal.

14

When I got back to Faslane, I messaged Philly.

> *Happy New Year! Hope 2013's a good one. It's been a while – how are you? How's life treating you? All good here, was just at my parents' for the break. Mum's been ill but she's on the mend, thankfully. Would be good to see you soon. x*

She answered the next morning:

> *Ollie! Happy New Year! So lovely to hear from you. I'm sorry about your mum – is she okay? I'm glad she's better. Things are good here, same old really – I saw Auntie Mel over the break, she says hi. She called you 'that nice shy boy who had a crush on you', which I thought you might appreciate. Definitely let's catch up soon. When are you coming to London?! It misses you. xx*

We made plans to meet in February, when I could come down for the weekend. She booked a show at Sadler's

Wells – a modern reinterpretation of *Giselle*. 'You don't mind going to a ballet, do you?' she said. 'I've heard it's great.'

We hadn't seen each other for almost three years. We met by the Tube, and when I stood before her, I had the same feeling I'd experienced on seeing her at Shane's: that she had grown into herself, in the most beautiful way. She walked up to me with a shy smile, her beige coat ending at brown boots that came up to her knees, her long hair tucked behind her ears, and time slowed down.

We went for a bite at a pizza place nearby. I was hyperaware of all my movements, my fingers fidgeting with the tablecloth, how intensely I pored over the minimal menu, my uneven breathing. When I finally looked up, I saw that Philly was peering over the menu as well, the slightest shake in her hands. She met my eyes, and her face relaxed into a dazzling beam. The waiter brought our bottles of beer.

'By the way,' Philly said, pouring hers into a glass, 'you *lied* to me.'

'What?' I said. 'What do you mean?'

'When we were little. You told me beer tasted like honey. I was so excited to try it. Thinking it would be this delicious, sweet nectar. I can't tell you how disappointed I was when I had my first proper beer.' She shook her head, laughing.

'I don't know why I said that!' I said. 'I was trying to impress you, I guess? I remember, even as I was saying it, I knew it wasn't true.'

'Do you remember what else I said, after?' she asked.

'Yeah. You asked me if I'd go to the Shield to drink beers when I got older. Which I did, by the way. Until I moved out.'

'It was so baffling to me at the time, how that could be a fun thing to do. Like, just sit around with someone, drinking. But, hey, look at us now, right?' She tilted her glass. 'You were right,' she said. 'We just had to wait and see.'

Our pizzas arrived, and she told me more about her doctorate. She was studying the impact of climate change on ecosystems. 'I'm hoping to finish next year,' she told me. 'And then, who knows? There are some post-docs I'd like to apply to.' She took a bite of her pizza. She folded each slice in two before eating it, like they did in New York movies to stop it dripping grease. I gave it a try too.

'How's Josh?' I asked.

'No idea,' she said, amused I had asked. 'We broke up three months ago. When he moved to South America.'

'Oh,' I said. 'That's a shame. Seemed like a nice guy. From what you've told me, at least.'

'He was alright,' she said, putting the rest of her slice down. She wiped her hands on her napkin. 'But it's not like we both didn't know it was coming. We were so different, him and I.'

'In what way?'

'It was like . . . Oh, I don't know. Maybe you'll think it's stupid. But do you ever feel like you can spend days and days with someone, and yet when they're not there, you don't miss them at all? Sorry, maybe that sounds too harsh. I really did like him. I loved him, even, in some ways. But there was always something a bit hollow about our relationship. Like no matter how hard we tried, we could never quite get to the core of each other.' She looked at me, then at her slice again. 'I guess, what I'm trying to say is, I want to be with someone whose absence I feel.'

I told her I understood. Under the table, our knees brushed briefly, a shiver passing through us as they did.

'Do you want my pizza crust, by the way?' she said, putting it on my plate. 'I never eat them.'

'Okay,' I said. 'Thank you.'

'What about you,' she said. 'You seeing anyone?'

'No,' I said. 'Not exactly easy for me to meet someone.'

'You will, though. You'll see.' She crossed and uncrossed her legs. 'But you've been in love, yes?'

'Not really,' I said, biting into her crust. 'I was dating this girl for a while at uni, in third year. Lea Mann. Maybe you knew her. But I guess it was similar to you and Josh. I didn't really miss her, when we were apart. It would have been nice to fall in love. I did try, if that makes sense. To picture myself loving her. But I couldn't.'

'There's nothing lonelier than that feeling,' she said. 'Of trying to love someone, without managing to.'

We finished our meal quickly, and despite my protest, she insisted we split the bill. We arrived at the theatre as the bell signalled us to take our seats. The hall was crowded and we battled our way to the second circle, up three flights of stairs. Our seats were high and in the middle of the row, and they gave us an overview of the space.

'Sorry, I know they're not the best seats,' she said. The room was plunged into darkness and the chatters around us stilled.

'They're great,' I whispered. 'We can people-watch.'

We didn't say a word throughout the ballet, enthralled as much by the dancers as we were at being so close to one another. I could feel Philly next to me, our shoulders touching, our hands lingering on the arms of our seats. The stage lights brightened her eyes, the shimmer on her lips, and when the show ended, I realised I had wished for it to last infinitely.

Unbeknown to us, it was the last performance of the leading ballerina ahead of her retirement. At the curtain call, she wiped away tears, and the crowd roared and clapped and threw roses at her feet. The director of the theatre presented her with a bouquet, and she gave another bow. She turned to embrace her husband, who was one of the dancers, and then he disappeared backstage and returned with their child. He must have been around one, not quite able to walk yet, and when he saw his mother his arms reached for her, and she gave him a kiss on the forehead. Yet when the husband sought to hand the child to her, she shook her head and turned back to the clamouring audience. She curtsied a final time, her hand on her heart, until the curtain closed.

'That was a bit odd, no?' I told Philly, as we got up to leave.

'What was odd?'

'The way she reacted. Like she didn't want to hold her child.'

An air of surprise crossed Philly's face. 'No, I don't think so,' she said, shrugging. 'She was working. It was her last performance. Not the time nor place for it.'

'But isn't that a moment you'd want to share with your family? The culmination of your career.'

'Maybe,' Philly said. 'Or maybe she just wanted to be a dancer in that moment. Not a mum.'

We went for a drink in Exmouth Market. Once we were sat by the bar, Philly asked after my parents.

'Mum's got one last round of chemo.' I pictured my

mother again, the hollows between her bones as I hugged her. 'I wish I'd been around for her treatment more.'

'You can't blame yourself for that, Ollie. You didn't know what was happening.'

'But I wasn't there for her and Dad.' The bar had begun to empty, falling into a lulled, peaceful state.

'I know what you mean. Every time I go home, I feel bad that I don't do it more often. But it's part of growing up, isn't it? We have to let go of our parents a little, while we build our own lives.'

'Yeah,' I said. 'I'm starting to realise that.'

We ordered a last round, and I talked about the stories my mum had told me over Christmas, by the fire. 'It's funny. She never said much about her childhood. But it was like she couldn't stop. I feel as if I've learnt more about her in two weeks than I had in twenty-six years.'

Philly fixed her gaze on the bartender cleaning glasses, a carefree smile on her. 'Maybe it's like the ballerina,' she said. 'Maybe it was important for her then, that you saw her as more than just a mum.'

I walked her to the Tube station. 'I'm going the other way,' I said, as we reached the escalators. She turned towards me suddenly. 'It was really good to see you,' I said. I reached for a hug, and I felt her body stiffen. I pulled away, my hands staying on her back, and I saw that she was frowning.

'Where are you staying?' she asked.

'Near Waterloo. There's this hotel where sailors can get really cheap rooms. Nothing fancy. But it's alright.'

'Okay,' she said. I waited for her to continue, forgetting to breathe.

'I just assumed . . .' she said.

I wanted to ask if she would like to come with me for one last drink. I wanted to ask if I could take her out again sometime, if she'd visit me in Faslane, or at the village even. I wanted to ask what would she do if I took her in my arms, what would she do if I kissed her. But instead of saying all these things I stayed mute, afraid of ruining the evening with unsought words. After a pause she turned back to me, her expression warm again, her hazel eyes dark in the night. 'Well,' she said. 'It was really good to see you, Ollie.'

'You too,' I said. 'Let's do it again soon.'

'Sure. Message me when you're in town.'

She hesitated an instant, and then she reached for my arm and gave it a gentle squeeze, gazing at me tenderly, sadly. She stepped onto the escalator, waving as she went down, and I watched her until she disappeared. Afterwards I made my way to the other side of the street, and the soft touch of her hand on my arm remained, holding on to me.

By the summer, Mum had made a full recovery. I went home and we celebrated at the Shield with almost the whole village. She'd regained some of the weight she'd lost and she'd put some make-up on, her lips a bright red. Her hair, which was growing thicker and frizzier than before, was wrapped in a yellow and green silk scarf I'd given her. Children of the village were running around the garden, tugging at her dress, and despite her tiredness she followed them wherever they wanted to take her, holding their tiny hands for support.

I thought again of what Philly had said: *We have to let go of our parents, while we build our own lives.* I pictured myself as one of those children, clinging to my mother's hand. I imagined my fingers slipping away from hers until they let go completely and I was free-falling to unknown territories. As I fell further away, I realised it wasn't just my mum I was letting go, but my whole childhood: the village and my father, my toys and my books, the cars in the garage. All of these things, which had once been my entire world, becoming fainter and smaller until I could barely see them, like stars whose light could no longer reach me. And I thought that the only way to make sense of this fall, the only way to assign value to it, was for wherever I ended up to be astonishing in its brightness.

PHOENIX MISSION
Commander Oliver Ines's Personal Log

Talos, Day 1583. Some tension on board.

We can just about spot the wreckage with our own eyes now. Every time I catch sight of it, I feel jittery. What an astonishing discovery this could turn out to be.

Even though Lucia agreed in the end, she's made a point of showing she did so reluctantly: retreating to her room, giving us the silent treatment at random, eating meals on her own. I'm trying to be as friendly as I can with her, but I find her behaviour childish.

'She'll be fine,' Shane told me. 'I'm sure she wants to see it, deep down.'

We were playing pontoon in the control deck. He's letting his hair grow this year, and now has it tied into a bun, which we've been teasing him about. 'I mean, the four of us, we're not exactly the most risk-averse, are we?' he continued. 'We're all lunatics, really.'

'I prefer Dom's word,' I said. 'Dreamers.'

'Yeah. Sure. That's the NovaTech-approved version.'

We played for a few minutes longer. I kept having bad luck with my draw, and within a dozen rounds Shane had taken most of my 'tokens' (we have A-T keep a digital score).

'You know,' he said, 'I've unlocked a new fear. It started as a bit of a joke in my head. But now I can't stop thinking about it.'

'What is it?'

'Well, what if when we come back, after ten years, Earth is abandoned? You know, *Planet of the Apes*-style. Like, I don't know. What if everyone's been nuked or there's been a meteor or something, and it's just the four of us in an apocalyptic world? What would we do?' He shuffled the cards as he said this, despite having done so already.

'Shane,' I said, 'you've got to stop watching sci-fi.'

'Fine. But look me in the eye, and tell me you haven't considered this scenario.'

'I haven't,' I said. 'It's ten years, Shane, not ten thousand. We'll be fine, I promise. Chances are, the world won't even have changed that much. It'll still be the same politicians, same music, same films . . .'

He remained dubious. I said some more reassuring words to him, nothing groundbreaking, until slowly our conversation took on a more relaxed tone. Finally, we went back to our cards. He seemed in a jollier mood, as if he was glad to have got this anxiety off his chest, as wild as it might have been. We ended up having quite a pleasant afternoon together.

At dinner, I was glad to see Lucia join the group – though she addressed only Dom and Shane, not me.

15

The next few years unfolded in a similar way, between the village and Faslane and *Valiant*, a weekend here and there in London, without my taking much notice of them going by. I was on my way to becoming lieutenant commander, made a decent living, got on well with my team and superiors and had access to some of the most advanced technologies. The work was demanding, yes, but I was beginning to spend less time at sea, and more in the office. I could visit my parents and friends, read one or two books a month, go on a date now and then.

Some of the novelty of the Navy had worn off, the missions on *Valiant* starting to feel repetitive. In January 2016 I turned thirty, and boredom became restlessness. I'd recently broken up with Lydia, a dental officer I'd met at base. Like most of my previous relationships, there was not one particular reason, but myriad minor ones that led us to fizzle out after three months.

I was single, and I could see the next decade mapped out in front of me. In a few years I'd be made commander, then captain, and then perhaps have a desk job at the Ministry of Defence. When I pictured this life, it didn't fill me with joy, but rather a nagging voice at the back of my head that kept saying, Is that all?

I thought that moving out of Faslane would help. I rented a one-bed flat in Glasgow, less than an hour's drive from base. It was nothing to write home about – the kitchen was old and grey, and the place had a worn-out sofa, cracking paint and cigarette burns on the carpet. There was a patch of mould on the bathroom ceiling that, no matter how hard I tried, I never managed to get rid of. I quickly settled into a new routine, and I've often wondered if I'd have kept going that way if Philly, Shane and Liv hadn't come to visit, in that autumn of 2016.

Philly had graduated the year before and was now part of an ecology research group in Edinburgh. It must have been cold – I have a distinct image of her shivering in a big coat and scarf, her hands in her pockets, as she entered my flat. Last time I'd seen her was a year before, at her graduation drinks. She'd been swamped with well-wishers and family, and I'd left after only exchanging hellos, in a rush to catch my train.

'Ollie,' she said, surveying the sparse living room. 'This looks like the house of a serial killer.'

'I haven't had time to decorate.'

'I should've brought you a plant or something. But I got wine instead. Here.'

She handed me the bottle. I went into the kitchenette to get a corkscrew.

'How've you been?' I asked.

'Good. Getting the hang of things in Edinburgh. My colleagues seem nice. I've made friends with one girl – I think we might rent a flat together next semester.'

'I'm lucky. Glasgow's cheaper. I could get a one-bed.'

'Oh, it's not even so much that. I like living with other people. I like the company.'

'What does that say about me, huh?'

'Well,' she said, 'to be fair, you do live with about a hundred flatmates for half the year. I'd probably fancy some quiet time, if I were you.'

'Right,' I said. And then, after some hesitation, I added, 'Do you think that's mad?'

'What?'

'Living in a submarine. My job. The Navy and all that.'

'No,' she said. 'Not mad at all. I mean, it's not something I would do. I'd get too claustrophobic, for one thing. I don't know how you do it. But I get it. It must be a thrill, in lots of ways. Why do you ask?'

'Oh, I don't know,' I said. 'I've just been thinking a bit about it, lately. What the next chapter's going to look like and all.'

The doorbell rang. 'To be continued,' Philly said. 'I'll get it.'

'Who would've guessed that *Ollie* would be the one to organise a reunion, huh?' Shane said, patting my shoulder. 'The most antisocial guy in our department.'

'Oh, come on,' I said. 'I wasn't *that* bad.'

Shane was a Chinook helicopter pilot now, in charge of evacuating casualties from conflict zones. He'd recently come back from a tour in Afghanistan. He told us snippets of his time there, as we ate the spaghetti I'd made with sauce from a jar – I wasn't a great cook. I wanted to learn more about his experiences. He made some jokes about his tour that bordered on the distasteful, while not really answering any of our questions. I wondered if he was like me, trying not to divulge confidential information. Under the table, he and Liv were holding hands, like teenagers: they'd just moved in together.

After lunch, we walked to the city centre and into a pub. Philly and Liv went to the beer garden to find a table while Shane and I ordered drinks. Shane got the first round. 'For that money I owe you,' he said.

'What money?'

'Our bet. The HEPHA mission. *Pegasus* – it launched last month, didn't it?'

'Oh, right, yeah,' I said. 'I can't believe Massey's actually done it.'

'Massive game-changer. For space, but for us too.'

'I know. He's advanced the tech by a good fifty years, I'd say.'

'Do you think you'll stay?' he asked. 'In the Navy, I mean.'

'Oh, I don't know,' I said. 'I was just telling Philly about that, before you arrived. Things are going well, and I have this flat now, so I'm staying put for the time being. But I'm getting the itch to try something new.'

'I know,' he said. 'Next year, I'm beginning to train new pilots. Me, a teacher, can you believe it? I'm not that fussed, if I'm honest. I'd rather be up in the air. And then they'll replace me, and I'll be put with all the other oldies in an office somewhere.'

'Yeah,' I said. 'But it's not too bad, for now.'

'Not too bad?' he said. 'You're being modest. Aren't you about to become, like, the youngest lieutenant commander in the Navy?'

'No,' I said. 'Well, I don't know. It's not like I've asked.' He scoffed, incredulous. 'By the way,' I said, trying to change the subject, 'you know you'd said two hundred quid, right? For HEPHA. Not a round.'

'Yes,' he said sheepishly. 'I shouldn't have brought it up, really.' His phone buzzed on the table. 'It's Liv. They've got a table at the back of the garden.'

Just before he locked his phone, I caught sight of his wallpaper. It was an abstract painting I'd never seen before, filled with splashes of red and soil-colour brown, bursts of oranges throughout.

'What's that?' I asked. 'Who's it by?'

'Oh, that?' he said, embarrassed. 'It's nothing, really. It's just . . . Well, since I came back from Afghanistan, I've been doing a bit of painting. I'm not very good. But Liv read somewhere that it could be good, you know.' He chuckled, glancing at me. '*Therapeutic*, she said.' He shrugged, his eyes on his phone. 'She bought me some brushes and acrylics and canvas, and I started messing about. And, well, it's been alright.'

Absentmindedly, he showed me some more photos. Always those reds and browns, some darker than others, some with glimpses of yellow and white, others struck with shades of grey and black. There was an urgency to them, an anger that you could detect in the sweeping and thick streaks of paint, in their chaotic alignment.

'They're great,' I said. 'You're pretty good at this.'

'Not really,' he said, nervous. 'But . . . well, yeah. It's been nice.'

He lingered on one image in particular. On it you could just about make out buildings and thin lines high above that resembled planes, and again those bright bursts of yellows and oranges and reds, against a darkened sky. Suddenly, he shut off his screen. 'Shall we join the girls?' he said, picking up our beers, and I followed him into the garden.

Shane and I have never revisited the talk we had about the HEPHA mission. It feels odd to think of us talking about it in such a casual way. But when *Pegasus* launched, it really did seem like its course was assured. Like with the *Challenger* launch, I sometimes return to videos of that day. Commander Masuda and his crew waving to the press, entering the craft. Inside they are at ease, having rehearsed this moment for years. When Masuda takes his seat, before securing himself you see him reach inside the breast pocket of his suit. He pulls out a photograph of his two children and his wife sat in the grass, squinting at the sun. You see the photo, very briefly, and you see Masuda admiring them, if only for half a second, those faces he knows as well as his own. You see his solemn expression, his lips pinching together as he tucks the photo back into his pocket and fastens his seatbelt.

How were we supposed to know what would happen? We saw *Pegasus* lift high into the sky, reaching orbit, heading towards the stars, and we cheered for them, for science and progress. Though I suppose we never did find out what happened, since the wreckage was never recovered.

But Mark has always been a cunning man: he announced the disappearance of *Pegasus* on the same day as voting closed for the 2016 US election. Commander Masuda and his crew were relegated to minor subheadings, not even their picture, not even their full names, simply the rather crude strapline, MASUDA AND CREW PRESUMED DEAD AS NOVATECH SPACECRAFT GETS LOST.

I saw the subheadings, and I thought of Commander Masuda reaching for the photograph in his pocket. I imagined his children and his wife looking at him adoringly through the rays of the sun, his face barely visible through the blazing light. And then I thought of my younger self in the car on the way back from Jimmy Lovett's birthday party, looking adoringly at my mum as she tried to make me laugh, her hair almost red in the light, the sun behind her blinding me. I thought of how our calcium, our iron, our nitrogen all come from the remains of stars' demise trickling through to us, I thought of how we were all made of stars. And I thought of how, really, the HEPHA team hadn't died or got lost; rather, they had returned to the place from which they had sprung.

16

After the pub, we walked Shane and Liv to the station. We said goodbye with promises to see each other again soon.

'Always so nice to see them,' Philly said, as we left the station. 'It's funny to see Shane all loved up like that.'

'I never pictured him as the romantic type,' I said.

'Liv fancied him at uni. She'd be so upset, when they were flatmates, and he'd bring back girls.'

We walked for a little bit, as I wondered what to suggest next. She hadn't said if she wished to drive back to Edinburgh straight away, or stay in Glasgow a while longer. I didn't want to assume anything. She looked at her watch. 'I'm not in a hurry,' she said, as if she'd read my mind. 'Do you want to grab a bite?'

We got a takeaway from an Indian restaurant and went back to mine.

'What were you saying about the Navy, this morning? When you asked me if you were mad to spend half your life down there.' She took out the food from the plastic bag.

I thought for a second. 'It's funny, Shane asked me as well, if I was having doubts about it. It's like I can see it all laid out, the promotions and climbing up the ranks, but I'm not sure it's what I want, really.' I handed her some plates and cutlery, which she set on the coffee table.

'Well,' she said, 'at least you'll be spending more time on land, the further you climb up those ranks. That's pretty good.'

'Yeah,' I said. 'But sometimes, I feel like maybe there's more. When I joined, it was all so exciting. The submarine, the new technologies, serving my country. But now, if I look back at the last eight years or so, I don't feel I have much to show for them. And that maybe there's something better waiting for me out there.'

She smiled. 'Do you remember the New Forest cicadas?'

'How could I forget?'

'Well, remember – they spend years buried underground, and then their last spring they come up to the surface, sing like crazy, find a mate and lay their eggs.'

'And then they die,' I said.

'Shh. Forget that part. What I mean is, maybe you feel like you're buried underground and you're waiting for something to happen. I felt the same way when I was doing my PhD. I kept thinking, am I wasting my twenties studying bugs at the same uni I've been at for almost a decade? But now . . . well, I love my job. And I realised I wasn't wasting my time. And you're not either, you know. You're growing, you're learning. When you least expect it, things will change for you. You'll find your calling, you'll see. It fits my Grand Theory of Life.'

'And what's that?'

'That in life, you've got transition years and action years. And the transition years might feel frustrating, because you feel you're just twiddling your thumbs . . . but, really, they're setting you up for the action years. The years when you feel everything is happening all at once. Because that's how it usually goes, don't you think? Nothing's going on, and then everything is.'

'Yeah,' I said, 'that's true actually.'

We began eating. The sun was fading, and I got up to turn on the light.

'Have you found them, by the way? The cicadas.'

'Nope. They haven't been spotted in almost a decade.' She pondered this, filling her plate with dal. 'They must be like you, right now. Under the ground, itching to see the light.'

After dinner, we watched a film in silence, lounging on either side of the sofa, our feet not quite touching. Both of us kept unnaturally still, any movement, any sound a trespass, our senses heightened and attuned to one another. When the film ended, we let the credits roll. Philly shuffled her feet on the sofa, tucking her knees into her chest.

'I don't think I can drive yet,' she said.

'You can sleep here, if you'd like,' I said, perhaps too quickly. 'I can sleep on the couch. And you can have my bed, if you'd like.'

She sat there, unblinking, amused. 'You can be so hard to read sometimes, Ollie.'

'What do you mean?'

'Well,' she said, with irritation, 'right now, for example. I can't really tell if you're acting clueless on purpose. Or maybe you're just not interested. Or maybe you are, who knows, but you're scared. Scared that I'm not interested, I mean. Or maybe some other mysterious reason. It's just so hard to know sometimes, with you.'

Our gazes locked, an electric rush passing through me. Philly turned her stoic face away, standing up from the sofa. She began clearing the table, bringing the plates to the sink. She tied her hair in a ponytail and rolled up the sleeves of her shirt, not seeming aware of her actions. She looked lovely, I thought. She turned the tap on, grasped the sponge laying by the sink.

'I just . . .' I began, terrified to say the wrong thing. I got up slowly and moved closer to her. 'I wasn't sure, you know . . . I didn't want to assume . . .' I picked up the tea-towel and started to dry the plates. She passed them to me, her eyes on the sink.

'It's okay,' she said. 'Maybe you're right. Maybe it is stupid. It would make things complicated, I guess.'

'I'm sorry,' I said. 'I just wasn't sure what you wanted from this evening.'

She turned to face me. 'Well, what did *you* want?'

When I didn't answer, she continued, 'I don't know, Ollie. Sometimes, when I see you, I feel so close to you. Like we were meant to be in each other's lives. Like we were meant for each other. I know, that sounds corny, doesn't it? I hate that I feel like that. Because at other times, I feel like you don't care about me at all. Like you don't care about us. Like if I stopped messaging you, that would be the end of our friendship. The end of us. And frankly, that makes me feel like shit.'

She went back to the sofa, and I followed her. She laid her head on my shoulder.

'Sorry,' she said. 'I didn't mean to get so annoyed.'

'It's okay,' I said. I put my arm across hers, carefully. 'Of course I care about you.' She waited for me to go on. 'Of course I'd wondered if we could be more than friends,' I continued. 'I've thought about it a lot. But I wasn't sure you'd want to be with someone who's unreachable for months at a time. Although I'm spending less time at sea now. And if you want, well, I'd really like that. For something to happen between us, I mean.'

She lifted her head from my shoulder and studied me, guarded. 'Okay,' she said. 'I'd like that too.' I brushed away a strand of hair that had fallen on her cheek, and I felt the softness of her skin. She took my hand into her palm, a nervous smile on her face. And as the film credits came to an end, there on my worn-out sofa, Philly and I kissed for the first time.

I woke up before her the next morning. She lay next to me, her hair spread across her pillow. I edged closer, kissing her neck. She turned her body towards me and opened her eyes, a wide beam appearing as she took in my face.

'Do you have an extra toothbrush?' she asked, putting her shirt on.

'Sure,' I said. 'You can take my travel one.'

'Thanks,' she said. 'Do you mind if I use your shower? Think I might have to drive straight to uni. I have a meeting at eleven.'

I opened my fridge and cupboards, checking what I had for breakfast: a bit of porridge, dregs of milk and an over-ripe banana. I could hear Philly humming in the bathroom. 'I'm going to run down to the bakery,' I told her, through the door. 'I'll be back in ten.'

'You're not running away, are you?' she said.

'No. Just getting you a croissant, that's all.'

I didn't have a fixed spot for my keys in the flat yet, and I never managed to put them in the same place. I checked my coat and jeans pockets, the kitchen counter and the sofa. I lifted Philly's handbag on the coffee table. And then, as I unearthed my keys hidden underneath, from the bag fell a transparent case which had her contact lenses, some cotton pads and make-up remover, and a green travel toothbrush. I placed it all back, careful to leave it exactly as before. I ducked out of the front door and headed to the bakery, smiling to myself, her humming in my head.

A year later, in the late summer of 2017, we were married in the village church. It was an unfussy ceremony: neither of us wanted a lavish wedding, and I'd just come back from four months at sea. My mum picked flowers from our garden in the morning, roses, dahlias and marigolds, and fashioned them into a bouquet. Shane was my best man, and my father acted as the unofficial photographer. Mrs Tan was there too, in her eighties with a cane at her side, sandwiched between Liv and Mr and Mrs Burns. Philly appeared in the nave, teary-eyed, arm in arm with her dad. When I caught sight of her I thought she was the most beautiful anyone could ever be, and I thought that all was right with the world.

We had the reception at the Shield, where the rest of the village joined us, and danced until the early hours of the morning. Once we could barely stand, we gathered our closest friends and family and made our way to the hill east of the village, not too far from the railway track. From there, we watched the sunrise. I put my jacket down on the grass so that Philly could sit without staining her white dress, and I held her close to me. Shane opened a bottle of champagne and he and Liv filled everyone's glass. My mum and dad huddled together, watching the scene unfold with serene faces. There was laughter, children running up and down the hill, the sound of more champagne opening. And now, my memory must be playing tricks on me again, for in my mind I see the sun, rising in all its glory. But when I look at photos from that morning, Philly and I on top of the hill, both of us grinning from ear to ear and our hair dishevelled, I see that the sky is shrouded in fog.

In a great demonstration of Philly's Grand Theory of Life, it was only a few days later that I was officially promoted to lieutenant commander. And it was not long after that, during our honeymoon on a little island in Greece, that I received the call from Mark Massey.

PHOENIX MISSION
Commander Oliver Ines's Personal Log

Talos, Day 1642. Some lingering stresses on board, mixed with high levels of anticipation.

We have a decent view of the wreckage now. We're almost certain it's *Pegasus*. I've asked Dom to bring us a tad closer for its details, its edges to become sharper. He hesitated for a minute, but after a short back-and-forth, he agreed.

Lucia has come around to the idea. Her irritable mood has lifted, thankfully. I caught her staring out at the wreckage earlier today, as she was coming back from the treadmill. The rest of us were sitting at the table, occupying ourselves by various means.

'If it really is *Pegasus*,' she said, 'what then? Do you think the crew'll be in there? Dead, obviously. But their bodies ... maybe they're still in there.'

'Maybe,' I said. 'From A-T's photos, it's likely there was some sort of explosion on the rear deck. So probably not. Chances are, they evaporated.' I examined the wreckage again, and my stomach churned. I don't know if the others feel it too. Something – someone? – emanating from it, something otherworldly that called to me, drawing me to its orbit.

'That's what scares me most,' Lucia continued. 'Not dying exactly. Honestly, if I die the day after we get back to Earth, obviously it would suck, but I don't really think I'd mind that much. No, it's dying up here that scares me. Dying alone, far from home, far from my family . . .' Her voice drifted away.

'Hey, it's okay,' Shane said, with a kindness that touched me. He gave her back a friendly rub. 'We're like a family too, remember? A really messed-up one.'

Lucia laughed. 'I know. You're sweet. But, come on, you know what I mean. I felt it as soon as we left. And when we couldn't see Earth any longer, I felt it even more. Didn't you as well? That feeling of being completely unbound, so far away. Of being completely on your own – of being lonely in a way I didn't think was possible.'

'Yeah, I felt it too,' Shane said. 'Poor Commander Masuda. Poor HEPHA team.' He paused for a second. 'What were their names again? The three others. What were they called?'

None of us could remember.

17

'You mean that really rich guy who lost all those astronauts last year?' Philly said, once I'd told her about the call from Mark, on our flight back to Glasgow.

'The HEPHA mission? Well, we don't know what happened. It could've been human error or something. Not necessarily to do with his spacecraft.'

'Sure,' she said, sceptical. 'And you're *positive* it was him? Not a scam? I mean, no offence, but why would *the* Mark Massey call you like that?'

'I thought it was a scam too! I hung up on them and just forgot about it. That's why I didn't mention it to you. But I got an email from his PA this morning. I checked the address and all that. It's really him, Philly. He wants to meet for lunch, apparently. In London.'

'Okay,' she said, making an expression that said, *I still don't really buy it*. She took my arm, using it as a headrest. 'How mysterious. Well, you should go. Get the most expensive thing you can order. See what he wants.

And then tell me everything, please. I want all the gossip.'

That evening, I looked up Mark Massey: he was fifty-two, married to his high school sweetheart, no children. It wasn't clear, exactly, how he'd made his fortune: a mix of old family money and good investments. He'd dropped out of Cambridge to build a betting app, which he then sold for millions, founding NovaTech soon after. The company was only fifteen years old, but already it had shaken the whole industry. In the eighties, following the *Challenger* disaster, NASA had discontinued its space shuttle model, leaving all space agencies to rely on Russian spacecraft. But then in the early 2000s Massey had come up with a refreshed model that was sleeker, bigger yet lighter and cheaper to produce, which had propelled the UK to become leaders of the space industry. Within a couple of years, they'd been adopted by NASA and the ESA, and JAXA had used them for the EROS mission to land the first humans on Mars. And now, despite the setback of the HEPHA mission, Massey's new nuclear model was once again creating a breakthrough across the industry that made space travel faster and more economical.

I had no idea how he'd found my details or how he had the slightest idea I existed. Later on, I'd learn that Captain Lowes had put forward my name, through some long-winded recommendation process. His call came to me as a huge surprise, but also as a signal I'd been unknowingly waiting for. He called, and I met him, and it was as if all the different fragments of my life came together with that missing piece, to create a coherent picture.

I took an early train to London, arriving before the appointment time. I walked around St James's Park for a while. It was raining and I bought an umbrella from a street vendor, not wanting to arrive dripping wet. I wasn't nervous, not really – curiosity had bested that. I suppose I had a vague idea that it would have to do with an engineering opportunity. I assumed he was one of those all-hands-on-deck, hyperactive CEOs who liked to meet all potential candidates. And, as I'd come to learn, I wasn't far off.

I waited for Mark in the lobby of his hotel in Mayfair – a grand, nineteenth-century building, with an imperial-style staircase and a crystal chandelier hanging over the foyer. I sat on an armchair in the corner. At exactly noon, a woman of about my age came to meet me.

'Oliver Ines?' she asked. 'It is pronounced "Eyenz", isn't it? Nice to meet you, I'm Louise. We've been emailing. Mark will be right with you. In the meantime, if you wouldn't mind signing this.' She handed me a piece of paper, and I skimmed through it.

'An NDA?' I asked.

She gave a courteous nod. 'I'm sure you understand.

Mark values his privacy very highly – and appreciates his guests to do the same. If you have any questions, though, please do let me know.'

I could tell this wasn't her first time giving this speech. What choice did I have? After scanning through the agreement as she hovered over me, I signed it.

'Thank you,' she said, taking the paper briskly from my hands. 'Mark will be here shortly.'

I waited for another couple of minutes. Classical music was playing, a piece I vaguely recognised. I heard the ding of the lift and its doors opening, and immediately I felt the energy of the room adjusting. The doorman and receptionists stood a little straighter, the porter shuffled away the luggage cart near the entry. Chatters became whispers, and eyes darted to the corner of the room by the lifts, where Mark Massey had appeared. He was shorter in person than I had imagined, and he looked older, too – but it was undoubtedly him. He saw me straightaway, and I stood up hastily.

'Oliver!' he said, as if we were long-lost friends.

'It's a pleasure to meet you, Mr Massey,' I said, enthusiastically. 'I'm a huge fan of your work.'

'Thanks,' he said. I detected a hint of a Northern accent which I hadn't heard when watching his interviews. 'You can call me Mark, by the way.'

We made our way to the top floor, to a private dining room, making small-talk.

Once we sat down, he asked me about my personal life. I was taken aback by his warmth. It wasn't often that I found myself being the talkative person in a conversation – yet, by the time we left each other, I had told him about my childhood and my parents, about Philly and Imperial and the Navy, while he hadn't disclosed anything about himself. Such was the way with Mark: he had the ability to draw you in, to give you the illusion that you were important and on equal footing with him, that you were sharing a moment that was heartfelt and real. But then he would leave, and you'd realise that while you were now an open book, he remained a mystery.

A waiter came in, placing in front of me the most delicious fish I'd ever had, buttery and tender and melting.

'So, what do you know about it, then?' Mark asked me, planting his knife in the flesh on his plate. He took a sip of his sparkling water: I don't think I've ever seen him drink anything else.

'I beg your pardon?'

'My work. You said you were a big fan.'

'Oh right,' I said. 'Well . . . I know that your nuclear thermal propulsion technology will allow spacecraft to carry larger cargo, which is crucial if we want to grow our presence in outer space more permanently. And it'll allow us to travel further into space than ever before, and for longer periods, too.'

He asked me some more technical questions, and I must have answered them to his satisfaction, as I sensed him ease his speech, as if I'd passed a test.

'You have experience with nuclear power, don't you, on *Valiant*? And I read your postgraduate thesis. It was good, actually. Interesting stuff. The bit about velocity, especially, it was perceptive.'

'Thank you,' I said. 'That was a long time ago, now, I—'

'Do you know what NovaTech is working on currently?'

I had the impression of being in a play for which only Mark had been given the script. NovaTech was working on thousands of things. They were working on Moon expeditions and HEPHA's successor, on probes and satellites and building new rockets with more reusable parts, and countless other projects. How was I supposed to know which one he wanted me to mention?

As if he'd read my mind, Mark continued: 'Well, I'm sure you do,' he said. 'You read the news, don't you?'

He waited for a moment, his eyes narrowing on me. A shiver went down my spine. He wanted to see, I think, if I would mention the HEPHA mission. I assumed it would be best not to.

'What's more interesting is what hasn't been announced yet,' Mark went on, quieting his voice, luring me in. 'Like Cilix.'

'Cilix?'

'Yes,' he said. 'The ESA and us, we're working on a probe to perform flybys of Europa. So we can know more about its geology, et cetera.'

He was looking down at his plate, yet I felt the full weight of his attention. I thought about the astronomy course I'd taken at Imperial, more than a decade ago now. I pictured Jupiter's moon, its smooth, pale surface patterned with streaks of red.

'You want to confirm,' I said, 'that beneath Europa's icy crust, there's an ocean waiting for us?'

'Bingo,' he said, not surprised at all – as if I'd simply said the correct line in his play. 'And if it does, the next step would be, of course, to see if that ocean could sustain life.'

We talked more about Europa and Cilix, and the work that was required – they'd only just begun building the probe, and I began to suspect that under the guise of asking for my opinion he was assessing my suitability for a job. As we reached the end of our meal – no dessert, never with Mark – he signalled to the waiter. 'Anyway, I enjoyed our chat, Ollie. And I trust you'll remember the paper Louise made you sign before I came in. She'll be in touch with you soon, to discuss certain matters.'

He walked me to the lift, its opening doors the curtain call of our play. Downstairs, Louise ushered me into a taxi, saying again that she would be in touch. Without me needing to ask, the driver took me straight to Euston station.

When I got back to Glasgow it was late, and Philly was asleep. I slipped under the covers as quietly as I could, but she stirred.

'How was it?' she whispered.

'It was alright,' I said. I had the NDA very much in mind.

She opened her eyes and sat up. 'Oh, come on! You have to give me more than that.'

'Sorry,' I said. I pretended to zip my mouth. 'I've been sworn to secrecy. But he was fine. A bit odd, but nice enough.'

'Odd how?'

'Pretty much how you'd expect the CEO of NovaTech to be. Like . . . he's always in full control of the situation.'

'Charming,' she said.

'Very,' I said, not sure if I was serious or not. 'Tell me more about your day.'

'It was good,' she said. She was doing research on a type of butterfly native to England that had begun relocating to a different habitat in search of cooler temperatures. 'You never see butterflies anymore. Have you noticed? Remember

Auntie Mel's garden? There were so many there. Now, you barely see any during the summer.'

'That's true,' I said. I pictured the butterflies leaving Mrs Tan's garden, their wings golden under the light, flying upwards and out of the village, in search of new places to call home. And then I thought about Mark Massey's spacecraft, sleek and golden as well under the light, leaving Earth to do the same. 'Maybe they'll come back,' I said.

'Yeah,' she said. 'I hope so. Anyway, it's late, my love. I'm going back to sleep.' She tucked herself into my arms, and soon after I heard the slow breathing of her slumber. I have always envied her ability to fall asleep within minutes.

When I woke up the next morning – a Saturday – I checked my phone. In my inbox, an email was waiting for me from NovaTech. I opened it without thinking, holding my breath. It was a job offer to work on the Cilix probe, as an engineer. I gave Philly a delicate nudge as I skimmed the details, excitement rushing in me. 'Philly, darling – wake up.'

'Huh?' she said. 'What is it?'

'NovaTech's just offered me a job.'

I saw her brain waking up, working out what I'd said, realisation dawning on her, and she beamed. 'No more submarine trips!' she said, chuckling, falling back into bed, her arms up in victory.

Within the hour, I'd accepted the offer.

18

Did Mark know from the start everything that would happen? Back then it had all seemed so natural, so spontaneous. 'Why don't you apply?' he asked me. 'It's pretty similar to the aptitude and physical assessments you had to do for the Navy, and only a marginally longer process.'

I felt so certain I had control. That when he asked me to apply to NovaTech's astronaut programme, in 2019, he did so unscripted, and that I was just one of many options available to him. And I was certain that when I gladly said yes, I had done so entirely of my own volition. But why else would he have wanted a submariner – someone able to spend extended periods of time in hostile environments – to join NovaTech to work on Cilix in the first place?

I can't ignore the possibility that Mark had designed my career at his company the same way he had designed his spacecraft. Patiently, minutely, and with a singular goal in mind. What that goal was, I hadn't worked out yet, but I now think it best described as mastery: of technology, of science, of the universe, of anything that was within his reach and, perhaps even more so, that wasn't. He sat there, slouched on a chair behind his glass desk, a view of all of London behind him, and he made me a proposition he knew I would have to be mad to refuse.

By then I'd been working on Cilix for two years. In less than two more, in late 2020, it would begin its journey to Europa. There was plenty riding on the launch: no craft, not even small probes like Cilix, had ever reached such a distant celestial body. Like the Navy, NovaTech operated in secrecy: I was given tasks on some of Cilix's parts, and I completed them, but much of the probe remained, to me, shrouded in mystery.

It was located in Surrey, a couple of hours from London. Philly and I'd moved to a house there, where she could continue her research. We had a garden, an apple tree occupying half of it, and on weekends we would take care of it together. Philly's fingers were greener than mine, greener than Mrs Tan's even. Everything she touched, everything she planted, flourished, sunflowers taller than us, roses so red they looked painted.

'You're already familiar with the workings of Nova-Tech,' Mark continued. 'We'd love to keep you. It would make sense for you to apply.'

No private company had ever launched an astronaut programme before, only government agencies. But Mark wanted his own. Construction of a NovaTech segment in the International Space Station – the ISS – was well under way, and his rockets were already sending people to the Moon and Mars. It was only logical for those people to be NovaTech employees and their findings to belong to him, and him only. That weekend, I checked the requirements more closely: *Demonstrable teamwork skills; sound risk management; a valid driving licence; a height between 150cm and 190cm and a BMI representing a normal body weight.* I met all of these conditions. Outside in the garden, I could see Philly reading by the tree, her back against its trunk, her legs outstretched. I went to sit next to her, telling her about my meeting with Mark. She listened attentively, waiting until I was done before speaking.

'You have to do it, don't you?' she said. She had sunglasses on so I couldn't quite read her expression 'Become an astronaut. Remember your star wallpaper? Remember that astronomy course you took at Imperial? It feels fated, somehow, doesn't it? And you've got the submarine training. They must have similarities, I'm sure.'

'I think so,' I said, relieved. 'I'd be stupid not to. But you know what it means, right? For us.'

'Yeah.' She smiled sadly, resigned to the situation. I looked down at her legs. 'Missions are usually, what, three or four months?'

'Sometimes six,' I said. 'But you don't go a lot. Most

astronauts, they do four, five missions in their career max, before retiring.'

'That's not too bad, my love,' she said. 'Nothing you and I can't handle.'

'Thank you.'

'For what?'

'Being there for me,' I said, my hand squeezing her thigh. 'Supporting me in all of this.'

'Well,' she said. 'You'd do the same for me, wouldn't you?'

'Of course. But we're getting way ahead of ourselves. I need to apply first.'

'I don't know,' she said. 'Mark obviously likes you, doesn't he? Feels like you have a shot. Otherwise, why tell you to apply? That'd be a waste of time for both of you.'

Dreamily, she pulled dandelions from the grass, fashioning them into a bouquet. 'And also,' she added, 'you *will* get it.'

'How do you know?' I asked.

'I just do,' she said, handing the posy of dandelions to me. 'I know *you*.'

―――

Everything I told her then was, to my knowledge, true. I really did think I would do one or two missions on the ISS, maybe one on our moon, but that that would be it. Since the EROS mission a decade prior, there had only been two other completed missions to Mars, and none planned by NovaTech: the failure of the HEPHA mission, Masuda and his crew's disappearance, had shrouded the planet in a hostile veil. And, yes, since I was working on Cilix, I had a vague intuition that Massey's next steps would be to venture even further afield. I can't deny the possibility he already had me in mind for the PHOENIX mission, but I certainly didn't know, not at that stage.

'Apply,' Philly said, 'and all the rest we'll figure out. It'll be an adventure.' But neither of us really knew how much 'the rest' would turn out to be. I applied to become a NovaTech astronaut and then I became one, and our lives entered a whirlwind. I had to go away often, to the Netherlands, Houston or Moscow, Montreal or Tokyo, to visit our partner space agencies, and learn more about the technologies and systems I would have to use someday. Or I'd be sent on extravagant training exercises in the most remote parts of the world. I'd be dropped in a cave or a forest for days to prepare me for isolation, the harsh conditions of space, and so that, if the spacecraft were to land in the middle of nowhere on its return to Earth, I would have the skills to survive until rescue came.

I spent my time gazing up at the universe, while Philly spent hers peering down a microscope or at a field, examining cells or organisms, uncovering all there was to know about them. We could spend days, weeks without seeing each other, or with only goodnights and good mornings. I don't think I turned a blind eye exactly, but I suppose it was easier for me to pretend that all was well, that we were strong enough to handle the distance, that Philly was content in our new life. It wasn't until we went to the Ahr valley, that I realised I had been mistaken.

It was about a year into astronaut training, in the late spring of 2020, when she came to see me in Cologne. I was attending a seminar with ESA astronauts at their nearby base, regarding a potential joint mission at the ISS, and we'd been given the weekend off. It had been Philly's 34th birthday the week before, which I had missed, and I wished to make it up to her. I suggested we take a day trip to the valley, to visit the vineyards.

We woke up before dawn and took the train to Altenahr. Philly fell asleep on my shoulder and I tried my best not to wake her, turning the pages of my book quietly. We made our way to the Red Wine Trail. All around us, hills were covered with grapevines, and small villages lay at their feet; in the distance you could see the forest, a backdrop of green. 'It's beautiful, isn't it?' Philly said. 'You don't get that kind of view in England.' We stayed looking at it for a little longer, and then she led me up the trail.

Though we were only in May, it was an incredibly hot day, which took us by surprise. The first hour went by blissfully. We hadn't had a free weekend for a long time, and we were enjoying being together, catching up. It was only when it got closer to noon and the sun was beating down on us that our moods shifted. We were dripping with sweat, barely any shade to protect us. Our conversation slowed, and soon after our pace did as well. Philly trailed behind me. When we were halfway up a steep hill, she came to a halt and crouched on the ground.

'It's too hot, Ollie,' she said.

'It's only a couple of kilometres until we reach the next village,' I said. 'We can get some shade there.' She took a swig from her water bottle.

'Didn't you think before suggesting this hike?' she asked me. 'Didn't you think it would be a bad idea in thirty-five degrees, without shade, sunscreen and barely enough water?'

'Sorry,' I said. 'I didn't know it would be this hot.'

'You didn't check the forecast?'

'Well, no,' I said. 'It hasn't been so hot this week. And I could ask you the same thing, no? You didn't think it was a bad idea either, did you?'

She shot me a look filled with reproach. '*You* suggested it!' she said. 'I assumed you'd plan it. I thought I would be fine to just go along with you. But you're right, that was my mistake. I should've known.'

'Should've known what, exactly?' I asked.

'I should've known you wouldn't be arsed to do the bare

minimum. That, as always, you'd come up with a big, grand idea, and I'd be the one having to deal with the dull practicalities. That I'd have to pick up the pieces.'

'Where's all this coming from?' I asked. 'What's the big deal? We can get to the next village and take the train home. It's fine.'

'It's *not* fine! It's always like this.' Another couple was coming up the hill, edging away as they passed us – but Philly didn't care. 'I'm the one who has to deal with the consequences of your actions. Do you realise that?'

'Philly, please,' I said, lowering my voice, 'if you want to have a go at me, fine. But can you do it when we're home, not in the middle of nowhere when, as you said, it's thirty-five degrees with no shade? Let's just take the train home.'

'Are you aware of all the sacrifices I've made for you?' she asked, ignoring what I'd just said. 'Do you think I wanted to leave Edinburgh and move to the countryside? My friends, my job—'

'You still have your job!'

'It's not the same! I don't have my colleagues. I don't have my office. You think it's nothing, right? That I'm being dramatic. But I gave up all these things to come here for *you*. For *your* job and *your* career and *your* life. And the worst part is, you're barely even at home! You're away half the time!'

She began crying and I stood there, melting under the sun, my heart breaking. I crouched next to her, and embraced her. 'I'm sorry,' I said. 'I know you gave up a lot for me. You know how grateful I am.' She sniffed into my shoulder. 'I guess I thought that, in a way, it was an adventure for you too. You said that, right? When you told me I should apply. I thought . . . well, I thought you were happy.'

'I am,' she said. A colony of ants was crawling between the vines, and she followed it with her eyes. 'But, Ollie, it's *hard*. You know it's hard for me, don't you? Even if there are some positives – they don't negate all the bad stuff. And . . . Well, I get lonely, sometimes.' She opened her bag and got out a packet of tissues. 'I'm not saying I regret it, or anything. But it's been a lot, hasn't it?'

'It has,' I said. 'For me too. It's been a lot of change.'

'Yes. But at least you get to go to space.' She got up, brushing soil off her legs. 'That's a pretty good compromise.'

'Yeah,' I said, getting up as well. 'That's true.'

She stared out at the valley. You could see the village nearby, the church's steeple towering over the tile-roofed houses. 'I'm sorry,' she said. Her voice quavered again. 'I just wanted today to go well. I just wanted us to have a nice day.'

'It's okay,' I said. I took her hand, and we climbed the hill. 'Every day's a nice day with you.'

When I asked her if I should apply, we didn't know everything that it would entail. We still saw the world as a field of opportunities, naïvely ignoring that with opportunities came surrenders. With her blessing, I applied to the astronaut programme. I put in a good word for Shane too, knowing Massey was keen to have RAF pilots. We did all the mental tests, all the physical tests, our bodies prodded and examined.

Once we'd passed the initial rounds, we began the training phase. We had lessons about the history of space exploration, science classes and survival-skills training. There were more tests and interviews, more assessments to see if we were strong enough, mentally and physically, in a process that took over a year. We'd started as nine thousand applicants, cut down to a hundred, then a dozen and finally, miraculously, three NovaTech astronauts, Shane, Ludo, who had also been an RAF pilot, and I.

I often get asked how it felt to be chosen as one of the three. And always I answer truthfully, that it felt surreal and humbling, thrilling and strange and overwhelming. But it made us feel something else, too, something that none of us knew how to put into words, not in a way that would sound quite right. What I don't say is that on top of all those emotions, being chosen as one of the three, after all those physical and mental tests, out of thousands of applicants, it made us feel like gods.

PHOENIX MISSION
Commander Oliver Ines's Personal Log

Talos, Day 1645. Wreckage confirmed by A-T to be *Pegasus*.

'Dom,' I said at our morning meeting, 'do you think we could move forward a tad more? If we get a marginally clearer view, we should be able to figure out exactly what happened.'

He caught Shane's and Lucia's eyes. 'I don't know, Ollie,' he said, hesitant. 'We're heading off course now. We know it's *Pegasus*. We know something went terribly wrong. Sorry if that sounds rude, but who cares what happened? That's not why we're here. That's not why we were dragged off Earth for ten years.'

'Agreed,' Lucia said. 'This was a fun side adventure, but let's go on to Europa now, please. I've had enough.'

I was disappointed by their lack of curiosity. Here was *Pegasus*, miraculously in our path, and all they wanted to do was forge ahead. I deliberated on what to say next. 'Look. This could have been us out there. This could be us. Dead, as Lucia said, with no one around, no one to witness our demise.' I pointed at the photo of the wreckage. 'They gave their lives for us, and we can't even remember their names. So, yes, I'm sorry for wanting to give them some of our attention. For wanting to understand their last moments. So that perhaps we can come back to Earth, having seen Europa, yes, but also being able to tell their families, their loved ones, that they're not lost, that we saw them here among the stars, and give them a bit of closure.'

'Very pretty,' Lucia said. 'But it's still a no from me, Ollie. And, honestly, let's face it, are you really doing this for them?'

'What do you mean?'

'Well, are we here for the HEPHA team, for their families, or are you doing it because you want to come back to Earth with not one but two breaking news stories? You want to come back all hero-like - hey, I found them! I found the missing astronauts from all those years ago. And, hey, I'm also the first man to walk on Europa, further than anyone's ever been. Take that, Armstrong. Take that, Masuda.'

'I don't know what you're talking about,' I said. And then I remembered we were not yet halfway through the mission. I couldn't let communication slip like this: I couldn't allow for insubordination. 'And I'd be careful, if I were you. I know we've been living together for almost five years, but I'm your commander. Don't forget it, please.'

'Oh, I won't,' she said. 'Believe me, you make that hard to forget.'

Before I'd had time to ask what she meant, Dom shushed her. 'Come on, you two,' he said, putting his hand on Lucia's shoulder. 'It's been a stressful few days.' He turned towards Shane. 'What do you think?'

Shane looked down at the floor, reluctant. 'I don't know, Ollie,' he said. 'You know me, I love an adventure. But is it really worth it, going so far off track? It's risky. And it'll add, what, a month to our journey? I don't really care for that.'

I considered what he'd just said. The atmosphere was tense, tenser than it had been in years.

'Think about Philly, man,' he said, so quietly only I could hear. 'Think about Tommy.'

No one said anything. I tried to calm my mind, to picture Tommy at home. Soon, he would turn ten. Soon he would have known an Earth without me for longer than he had one with me.

'Fine,' I said. 'Dom, get A-T to reroute us to Europa, please. But let's curve around the wreckage if we can. So we can get a different angle.'

They looked at one another, and I maintained a peaceful composure. Dom let out a small sigh. 'Aye aye, Commander.'

19

My first mission to space, to the International Space Station, was scheduled to launch on 10 October 2022. I was thirty-six years old. On the morning of the launch Philly, my parents and Shane came to wave me off. We were separated by a glass wall. Shane appeared envious – his first trip was not due until the next year. My father stood stiffly between Shane and Mum, and when I appeared in my uniform, for a split second I saw a proud grin on his face. My mum began tearing up and Shane went to her, making a joke or reassuring comment that I couldn't hear, and she let out a small laugh.

Philly was three months pregnant, and she was just starting to show. When the crew announced that it was time for us to go, she put her hand on the glass wall, her smile giving way to an expression of fear. For a brief moment, I wanted to break the wall and go back to her. She must have seen worry forming on my face, or guilt, as she mouthed to me comfortingly, 'It's okay.' I put my hand on hers on my side of the wall, and we stayed there for an instant, as everything around us blurred, as everything quietened to a whisper.

The launch remains perfectly clear in my mind. It took place at the Kennedy Space Center, in Florida. We were a crew of four, Ludo and I from NovaTech, Dom and our commander, Maddie, both from NASA. We lay on our backs in the capsule's flight deck, all strapped into our seats. We heard noises below us, as the engines ignited. An odd sense of emptiness came over me, and a calming focus. I thought about the boy I had once been, of late nights at the library and Saturday mornings in the garage with my father, of the Navy, *Valiant* and Cilix. I thought about everything that had led me to that capsule, as if contemplating an elegant equation. And I thought that everything made sense, that all of those past moments, bright ones and dark ones and some shaded in doubt, had brought me somewhere astonishing.

Ground Control began the countdown, and when it reached zero, there was a low, rumbling noise. Ludo and I locked eyes, and with a nod I tried to appease his apprehensive look. From the small glass window I saw smoke and the orange of the flames reflecting onto the clouds, and we were off. The sky became sombre and our bodies began to shake. The first and second-stage boosters exhausted their fuel and fell back to earth, exploding below us with loud bangs.

The ride became smoother as the air thinned and then, after only eight minutes and thirty seconds, another loud bang and a jerk as the last section of the rocket was jettisoned from the spacecraft. We were in orbit, and around us there was only darkness and silence. I no longer knew a minute from a second. Though my body was safely harnessed I felt it lift from my seat. Earth's gravity no longer anchored me. It was as if I was hanging upside down, no longer part of my home planet. Instead I belonged to something much bigger, much greater, I belonged to a limitless world. Maddie got up and floated to the control deck. 'Houston,' she said, 'preparing to dock.'

In some ways, the ISS was a less hostile environment than *Valiant*. After all, we weren't carrying nuclear missiles up there, and we could call and receive emails from home. I had some days of dizziness, yes, an upset stomach and a throbbing headache, but those discomforts settled down shortly. We slept in bags hanging from the ceiling with Velcro straps, which took me a couple of weeks to get used to. But overall, the excitement of the novelties surrounding me overwhelmed my homesickness.

The station was more cramped than you might expect. Each agency had their own laboratory module, more corridor- than room-like, and everywhere you looked there were wires, tech, handrails and grips to help us move around. Tatsuki from JAXA and Andrei from Roscosmos were conducting their own research, Lucia and Patrick, both from the ESA, were growing plants using a new, self-sufficient system. It used a minute amount of water to conduct electricity and produce artificial light, which was then recycled to water them. Meanwhile, the Americans were doing tests on cement, with simulated lunar soil, to see how the two reacted in free fall during the hardening process. It was no secret that NASA had begun work on building colonies on our moon.

Ludo and I were experimenting with robotics, using the gravitational field to test different mechanical systems. We were also assigned to trial a vest that made use of a new technology, to shield the most susceptible organs from radiation poisoning. The vest was bulky and stiff, and the others teased us about it, but they proved efficient: I have one on right now, and without them we wouldn't have been able to go that deep into Jupiter's radiation zone.

In early December, I did my first ever EVA – Extravehicular Activity, also known as a spacewalk. An antenna outside the station had developed a fault, and Maddie and I were assigned to replace it. We went inside the airlock to get ready. My hands shook slightly as I put on my suit. 'Are you scared?' Maddie asked. This was her third EVA. 'Don't worry. You've trained for this. It'll be a walk in the park.'

We began checks on our spacesuits, which took a while: one minuscule tear or leak would most likely prove fatal, so we had to be extremely thorough. They were, really, more like personalised spacecraft. Each suit had its own electrical, ventilation and communication systems, thermal control and drink bags. It was heavy and rigid, and its pressurised environment made moving about an odd and awkward experience, like walking under water.

At the back of our suits, tethers were safely hooked to the station, to stop us drifting away. 'Ready?' said Maddie.

I took a wide breath. Once again, more than fear I had a feeling of utmost focus – and the strange certainty that my whole life, somehow, had led me here, 420 kilometres above Earth. I found that thought soothing. 'Ready,' I said. Maddie opened the door to the airlock, and we stepped into the great outdoors.

Besides the hum of our suits' fans, it was noiseless. Underneath us there was Earth. I could see the sunrise right above it, a crescent-shaped sliver of light that grew larger and brighter, a halo in the dark. I saw the sliver grow, and the planet was immersed in its blaze. I could see in full colour the clouds enveloping it, the water and the earth. Below was the Atlantic Ocean, some mist swirling atop, like a hazy blanket. To our right was North Africa and mainland Europe, Portugal, Spain, France – and then, a little above us, slightly to the right again, there was

England. And I felt that if I looked a while longer, I'd be able to see Philly at home in Surrey, reading in the garden, resting against the apple tree. Ground Control spoke in my ears: 'Ollie, Maddie, we have visual. Ollie, take a step back to your left, and then go right. The spare antenna is stored just below.'

For five hours we were out there, Ground Control guiding our every movement, as the sun rose and settled upon Earth. The repair was not so different from what you might expect – drilling and bolting and ratcheting – except that our tools floated and the suit made it strenuous to carry out the simplest manoeuvre, the tightening of a screw or turning the antenna to point in the right direction. I'd be lying if I said it wasn't stressful. There was the exhilarating backdrop, yes, but also the knowledge that the only thing standing between us and a certain death was our suit and a tether.

At one point I was struggling with a particular screw, and even though the suit was regulating my body temperature, I could feel sweat forming on my forehead, sticking to my skin. This wasn't ideal, of course: any water in the helmet risked fogging the visor or impacting the suit's systems. We were still a while away from any of this happening but Maddie took the tools from my hand, and finished the movement for me. Afterwards time went by quickly, and in what seemed like only minutes we were back in the airlock, the EVA a success. I took in the scene one last time, the silence, the emptiness. I took in Earth below us, insignificant against the vastness beyond it, yet encompassing everything that I held dear, and everything that had led me away from her.

20

For Christmas, Philly and my parents had arranged for gifts to be sent to the ISS, smuggled onto a cargo craft in October. My mum, as she did every year, had knitted me socks, navy blue and white striped, to match my uniform, and sent them in a care package of chocolate frogs, Jammie Dodgers and Quavers. Beneath the layers of snacks, carefully wrapped in tissue, was a framed photo of Philly, me and our parents on our wedding day, standing in front of the church. I took in the scene, the rose petals and rice at our feet, our beaming faces, the way that Philly's dress draped on the floor in waves.

Afterwards, I opened Philly's package. And there in my hand was the magnifying glass from our childhood, not quite as heavy as I'd remembered, its lens scratched. On the wooden handle she had carved our initials and the date we had first met, that summer of 1995.

'Thank you,' I told her on a video call that evening. 'I love it.' She had gone to her parents' for the holidays, and behind her I could see the Christmas tree. Her bump was now fully visible, her hands resting on it, and though she was tired, she seemed in high spirits.

'Don't thank me, thank Auntie Mel,' she said. 'She helped me find it. It was hidden in her attic, somewhere.'

'Miracle she still had it, after all these years.'

'That's what I said! How's Christmas up there?'

'It's been good. We all had the day off. Dom and Tatsuki played some Christmas tunes on the guitar throughout the day. And then we watched *It's a Wonderful Life*.'

'Sounds dreamy,' she said.

'Not really,' I said. 'It would have been better to spend it with you.'

'You'll be here soon,' she said. She looked down at her bump. 'The little one's kicking like crazy. I can't wait for you to feel it, Ollie. It's really cute. And weird too.'

'Is it all going okay?' I asked, guilt pressing down on my shoulders.

'Oh, yeah, don't worry,' she said. 'My back hurts so I haven't been sleeping much. And my feet have doubled in size. But I'm okay. I just miss you, that's all.'

I felt most apprehensive during the trip when we were prepping for our descent: I'd been told many times that re-entry into Earth's atmosphere was the most complex and dangerous part of the journey. The difficulty lay in penetrating Earth's orbit. Once we entered it, Earth's gravity would begin to pull us towards it swiftly, while the particles of the atmosphere, now much denser, would slow us down. As we battled to push through the thick air, friction would arise, and the spacecraft would heat drastically. It was hence of the utmost importance that we entered the orbit at the right angle: too steep, and the friction would be too strong and would burn us all to a crisp; too flat, and we would bounce back into space, unable to break through the dense atmosphere, like a stone skipping across water.

We undocked from the station and began the descent. I had my head down, but from the corner of my eye I could see the whole capsule shaking. My whole body broke into a sweat: it was like being inside a fireball. After what felt like both an eternity and an instant, the parachutes opened and we slowed, landing in the middle of the Kazakhstan desert. All had gone exactly to plan, and I felt the tension leaving my body.

I came back from that first journey into space with a shifted outlook. I had witnessed how minute our planet was against the backdrop of the universe. I saw the paper-thin layer of atmosphere that guarded it, how trivial a day was amidst the eternity of its surroundings. I landed back on Earth, and everything seemed so frail and finite, as if we were nothing but ants eating away an apple, leaving only its core. But before I had even time to ponder this shift in great details, an even bigger revolution occurred for me.

It was the middle of the night, barely two months after my return to Earth, when I felt a shake on my shoulder. 'Ollie,' Philly said. 'I think it's time. Holy shit.'

'Time for what?' I said, half-asleep.

'The baby! Hello! It's here!'

I stood up in a jolt, rushing around to get the bag and the keys and the car. Twenty minutes later, we were in the hospital. The lights were blindingly white and the reception area was filled with drunken men and teenagers, loud and getting into fights, and there was an underlying smell of vomit. 'How relaxing,' Philly said, between short breaths. She was in her pyjamas, her face flushed red, her hair in a tangle. 'Exactly how I'd pictured giving birth.' Soon after, we were ushered to the maternity ward.

I couldn't say whether I found the EVA or Philly giving birth more stressful. Dr Yen and the nurses were rushing about, Philly uttering some curses and gripping my hand tightly, her parents and mine poking their heads in and then, seeing the chaos, deciding it would be best to wait outside. 'Almost there,' Dr Yen said. 'Just one more big push.' Philly pushed again, squeezing my hand to the bone and then, like the rarest of miracles and the most common of occurrences, there was life, and I became a father.

PHOENIX MISSION
Commander Oliver Ines's Personal Log

Talos, Day 1711. Back on track. Europa grows brighter, and *Pegasus* has all but disappeared.

As we approach the halfway point of the trip, the mood has taken a hit. We're all a bit snappy with one another. Shane gets annoyed at Dom's singing; Dom thinks Lucia chews too loudly; Lucia thinks Shane cracks too many jokes. I decided to give everyone the day off. And then, in the evening, as we were debating what movie to watch, it happened: a loud noise, and a slight shake.

'What was that?' Shane said. He went to the control deck. The rest of us looked around, concerned.

'A-T,' I said. 'Did you register unusual activity?'

A-T's screen lit up. 'Impact registered thirty-two seconds ago. Location: main engine deck.'

'Shit,' Dom said. We all realised, of course, that this meant the reactor.

I asked A-T some further questions. The impact had been light, probably caused by a micrometeorite that *Talos* had failed to detect. It's possible that this was caused by overriding the autopilot during the last few weeks, but we couldn't be sure – it was as likely to have been a minor fault, really.

'We need to investigate the damage more closely.' I said, ignoring everyone's stares. 'We need to do an EVA.'

'Really?' Lucia said. 'We're already pretty far into Jupiter's radiation zone.'

'Our vests and suits have been built for this,' I said. 'If we work efficiently, we should be in and out in a couple of hours. We'll plan it for after-tomorrow. That'll give us time to prepare. Lucia, get A-T to run the coordinates. Dom, you'll do the walk with me.'

Dom frowned. 'I'm sorry, Ollie . . . I want to. I will if you want me to. But, look. I've been meaning to talk to you about it. I've been experiencing some aching.' He put his hands around his stomach. 'Here.' An image flashed in my mind, of my mother making the same gesture, crouching in pain.

'What do you mean?' I said. 'How long has this been going on?'

'A while,' he said. I thought about our diminishing stack of painkillers, his face grimacing as he ate. 'I should have told you earlier, I know. I tried, right before *Pegasus*. But we kept getting sidetracked. At first I assumed it was indigestion, or something like that. But it hasn't stopped. And the last month or so, it's been a bit rough.'

I caught Lucia's eyes. We'd all considered the possibility of one of us getting ill. We could do minor procedures on board: we had received medical training, after all. But when we signed on for this mission, we knew that treatments or operations would be almost impossible. It was there in our contracts, black ink on white pages. It was just part of the job.

'You should have told me, Dom,' I said, trying my best to sound calm. I'll need to have a proper conversation with him later on. 'Lucia, can you run a medical exam on him? Shane will do the EVA with me.'

So much for our day off. The spacewalk will no doubt require us working overtime. We'll need to spend the evening preparing the suits and going through the route with A-T. The likelihoods are, we'll arrive at the engine deck, see there was no need to worry, and that the EVA would have been for nothing. But we can't take any risks. We're entirely reliant on the reactor, and if it has any sort of issue, if it misfires in any way - a leak, a meltdown, it would no doubt be catastrophic: the last five years will have been in vain.

21

On *Talos* this morning, I cleaned my locker. It's a mystery how my belongings seem to have accumulated over the years. I organised my clothes, my diaries, checking-in on Philly's note again, the note bearing her name, smoothing its edges. At the very back, hidden behind my jersey, I touched something soft and small. When I pulled it from the locker I saw it was Koopa, and I reminisced about the day we'd gone to the zoo, Tommy, Philly, my parents and I, in 2025.

We'd moved back to London, to a flat in Bermondsey, after Philly received a research position at UCL. I was slowly getting ready for my second mission at the ISS, due in six months' time. It was to be my first mission with Shane, and we were looking forward to it. NovaTech had just contracted with a French fashion house to design our spacesuits.

'What's his deal?' Shane said, after Mark had asked us what colour we'd want our suits to be. He never did like Mark very much. 'Who gives a shit what colour our suits are?'

'I guess it'll be good marketing for us.'

'I'd prefer him to pay more attention to the stuff that actually matters. Like, I don't know, making sure they work properly.'

'Are you talking about what happened to Ludo? He's fine. Only a minor problem with the filter. All fixed now.'

Tommy must have been two. He was a happy toddler. I see him running around the zoo enclosures, pointing at the animals, all of us trying to catch up with him. My father did impressions of each of the animals they came across, a lion's roar, an elephant's rumble, giving it his all, with farcical expressions and movements that made Tommy laugh until he coughed. My mother told him to tone it down but he went on, as other children and their parents turned to watch. I'd never seen my father like that. I felt as if I was intruding on a scene not meant for me.

'Your dad has softened since becoming a granddad, hasn't he?' Philly told me, as we trailed behind with the empty pushchair. A little further away, we could see the giraffe enclosure, and Tommy ran to it, my parents in tow.

'He has,' I said. I watched my father catching up with Tommy, lifting him high into the air. 'It's weird, seeing him like this.'

'I used to be scared of him when we were kids – when

I'd come to your house. But I'm glad Tommy's getting this version of him. It's sweet, no?'

'Very sweet.'

'Are you okay?'

'Yes, great,' I said. 'Why d'you ask?'

'I don't know. You just seem a bit distracted, that's all.'

'Sorry,' I said, 'I'm a bit tired. Lots going on at work.'

'It's alright,' she said, taking the pushchair from me. 'But, please, try to be *here*, you know? You're going back up there, soon.' She pointed at the sky. 'We need to treasure these moments.'

It's true that my mind was full at that time. It wasn't only Tommy who was growing at an incredible rate: the space industry was making rapid progress, too. Radiation-shielding technology improved and A-T's first model was introduced in early 2024. NovaTech had welcomed two new cohorts of astronauts, so that we were now nine in total. We learnt how to grow food more reliably and economically, and how to recycle water on board more efficiently. And it was my job to keep up with all these new and shiny technologies, to know them inside out and to inaugurate them in front of the world.

Not long before the day at the zoo, I'd had lunch with Mark. We met at the same hotel we had the first time, almost seven years prior. For all his obsession with innovation, Massey was very much a creature of habit. Even the fish was the same, buttery and tender, my fork slipping into its flesh.

'So, you're enjoying it?'

'Sorry,' I said. 'Enjoying what?'

'All of it,' he said quickly. 'Life, NovaTech, being an astronaut, this lunch.'

'Oh, yes,' I said. 'Very much so. All of it. Thank you. For the opportunities. And this lunch too, of course.'

'And you've been keeping track of Cilix?'

'I have, yes. It should enter Jupiter's orbit just before I go back on the ISS. And we should start getting some findings from its flybys around the time I land back.'

'Yes,' he said. 'I can hardly wait. Can you imagine? That little probe, whatever it reports back to us, might change the course of humanity. It might change our whole entire place in the universe.'

I nodded in approval, and he continued. 'But in a sense, Cilix is only the small picture.' He leant towards me, slowing down his speech. 'You must know what I mean, right?'

'I . . . yes,' I said. 'You don't just want to see if it can sustain life – you want to see if there *is* life.'

'That's right,' he said. 'But that's not all. What we really want to do with Cilix is to test the water, literally *and* metaphorically speaking. We've already observed that Europa has zones that are less radioactive than others, as you know. Where it might be possible for humans to land and explore. We want Cilix to confirm those observations, among some other things.'

'I see,' I said. I wasn't sure how privy I should be: as I've said, a lot of NovaTech's inner workings were not made available to me. 'So, that's the idea, then? Sending humans to Europa?'

'We're not quite there yet. But, yeah, that would be the end goal, obviously. Same thing we did with our moon and Mars. First we observe, then we send the probes, and then us.' He put down his cutlery. 'But Cilix won't be back until 2026, all being well. And then, even if we get a head start, it'll take another few years until we'd be ready to launch.'

'By a head start, what do you mean exactly?' I asked.

He turned to me, startled, as if he'd forgotten my presence, which I suspected was also part of his performance: feigning reflection, feigning idleness, when in reality he had planned this lunch to the minute. 'I mean that the technology is almost there, and that we've begun work on the spacecraft. The ESA, NASA and us, we're working together. We're providing the technology, of course, but they're funding parts of the mission.' He took a long sip of his sparkling water, putting it down unhurriedly. 'And I mean, that we could start training the staff before Cilix returns.'

A shudder came over me – of dread or excitement, or

most likely a mixture of both. I had had vague ideas about the future of NovaTech, yes, but so far, everything had remained within the realms of potential. It was only when he mentioned staff that I felt those blurry possibilities come into focus, my intuition turning into inevitability. I was a NovaTech astronaut. I was the staff that was supposed to go to Europa.

Mark fiddled with his fork. 'You see, one of the challenges is that it would be quite a long mission. Eight years, according to my estimates. So, we – the ESA, NASA, us – we'd need to send astronauts who are relatively young, in their early forties, at most. But we'd need to begin their mission-specific training years before because it'll be pretty gruelling, as I'm sure you can imagine.'

Something in my face must have shown anxiety, as Mark gave me a reassuring smile. 'Don't worry. This isn't a job proposition, if that's what you're wondering. I'm just, well, assessing my options. And I'll trust you'll remember that the NDA you signed is still valid.'

'You're right,' I told Philly back at the zoo. 'I'm here.' I gave her a kiss, and ran up to Tommy.

'Hey, little man,' I said, lifting him up. 'Why don't you give Granddad a rest? Where do you want to go next?'

His head turned in all directions, his tiny body wiggling in my arms, warming them. 'There!' he said, pointing at the gift shop. Inside, there were plush toys and puzzles, cards and notebooks and magnets. 'You can get one thing,' I said. 'You've got to choose carefully.'

'That one,' he said, with no hesitation whatsoever, pointing at a soft, green plush turtle, the size of my hand. 'You sure?' I asked. 'How about a lion, or a rhino?' He shook his head vigorously.

'Ollie,' Philly said, laughing. 'Let him have the turtle. It's cute.'

'Okay,' I said. 'We'll get the turtle.'

'What will you name him?' Philly asked him at the till.

'Koopa,' he said. Philly chuckled again.

'Koopa?' I asked. 'Where's that from?'

'It's from *Mario*,' she said. 'The turtles in *Mario*. They're called Koopas.'

'Oh,' I said, still rather confused. 'How on Earth does he know that?'

'We play, sometimes. Well, he watches me play, I guess. You know, when you're away. And we saw the movie too, recently. It was fun.'

Over the years, Koopa's green has paled, and there are a couple of loose threads hanging from it. I hadn't seen Tommy put it in my bag. Who knows? Maybe it had been Philly. But I like to imagine him sneaking into our bedroom as I was busy packing, tucking the soft toy between my folded shirts to keep me company on the journey. I pulled Koopa from my locker and gave it a squeeze. As I did I caught a whiff of Tommy's scent, of baby wipes and sweetness and milk, but all at once it was gone, replaced by the metallic smell of *Talos*.

I imagined Tommy again, slipping the soft toy into my bag, only this time, I saw his face filled with worry. The thought crossed my mind that perhaps he hadn't given Koopa to me so that it could keep me company. Instead, I wondered if he had been afraid that I would forget him, and that he had slipped the turtle into my bag as a fearful plea for me to remember him, and for me to return.

22

After the zoo, we went back to our Bermondsey flat for tea. We had an open-plan kitchen, and as I made everyone's cup I could see Tommy and Philly playing on the carpet in front of the telly, with Koopa and the other soft toys. Mum and Dad were on the sofa, watching them play. I waited for the water to boil. Mum moved in her seat, unable to find a comfortable position. My dad's eyes darted her way repeatedly.

'Mum,' I said. 'Are you alright?' Philly looked up. There was silence, even from Tommy.

'Oh, yes,' she said. 'I'm fine, thank you.' She caught my dad's eye.

'You sure?' Philly said kindly. 'If you're cold, we can turn the heating on.'

'No, no, I'm fine,' Mum repeated. 'It's just, well . . .' She bit her lip, turning to Dad again.

'Well,' he said. He took a deep, tired breath, his palm on Mum's hand. 'We wanted to tell you before we leave. Your mum's cancer, it's come back.'

I felt numb, like a soldier about to rejoin battle. On the floor, Tommy began calling for Philly.

'Okay,' I said, a shiver in my voice. 'How long has it been?'

'Dr Cosler told us last week,' Mum said. 'I start treatment on Tuesday.'

'It's more aggressive this time,' Dad said, shaking his head. 'It's growing more rapidly. But, well, it should be okay. It *will* be okay.'

Philly took Tommy to his room, glancing at me with worry. He began crying, his new toy in his hands, his shrieks reverberating across the flat, echoing in me. I felt the past catching up with me. I felt that no matter how far, how high I went, I would always be tethered to my home and the village – as a place to warmly fall back to, yes, but also, as a place that could, at any moment, violently pull me back towards itself.

———

When I came back from my second trip on the ISS, about a year later, the growth of the tumour had slowed. After a week of quarantine, I went straight to see Mum at the hospital, where she was undergoing chemo. When I came into her room she put on her dark blonde wig, backcombing it.

'You don't have to put that on to see me,' I said, hugging her, the hollows between her bones there once more.

'Oh, I know, darling. But it's nicer, isn't it? I don't want you to have this image of me in the hospital. I want you to see me how I was before.'

'I do. You don't have to worry about that.'

She asked about my trip. I told her that Dom had prepared an Easter-egg hunt all over the station. I told her about the spacewalk Shane and I had completed together, how even he had been lost for words seeing Earth like that, so fragile, so radiant. The painkillers made her drowsy and dizzy, and she struggled to keep hold of the conversation. 'So how's Philly getting on in Edinburgh? It's such a lovely city.'

'No, Mum,' I said, as casually as I could muster. 'That was a few years ago. We're in London now. She works at UCL.'

An air of confusion crossed her face, before it dawned on her. 'Oh, yes, of course,' she said. 'I know that. Sorry. It's been a long day.'

'Don't worry,' I said, as I pulled up her duvet. 'It's hard to keep up, sometimes. We've travelled a lot.'

'You were so sweet, you and her, that summer,' she said, with a faraway expression. 'Tied at the hip the whole of August. The first time she came to our house, I thought, There's a strange, sweet girl.'

'Why strange?' I asked.

'There was just something about her that was so . . . curious. You might have forgotten this. But for a while, by the corner of the living room, near the telly, we had a little cabinet there and I'd put a fern on top. And Philly, I can still picture her, barely as tall as the cabinet . . . I went to get you two some juice, and when I came back to the living room she was touching the plant's soil.' She reached for her glass, and I brought it to her lips, watching as she slowly drank. 'It was like she was stroking it,' she continued. 'Right there, on tiptoe, her fingers in the dirt. And then I realised she was checking to see if it needed to be watered! And that's when I thought it. There's a strange, sweet girl.'

'I don't remember seeing her do that,' I said. 'But, hey, it's not surprising, is it? You've seen our flat.'

'Yes. Plants everywhere. Like a mini jungle.' A tired smile arrived on her face, as a thought seemed to cross her mind. 'I'm glad you two found each other,' she said.

Not long after, a nurse came to tell us it was time for Mum's scan. I hugged her goodbye, making plans to come the next week with Philly and Tommy. I went to buy a coffee in the cafeteria, which was empty. I wanted to savour an instant on my own, to be held in a state where I had no obligations, no worries and neither a past nor a future. I had no service on my phone, and I sat there in the vacant cafeteria, drinking the watery coffee, looking into the void.

It was hard to tell if the story Mum had told was true, or if her medication was playing tricks on her memory. I chose to believe it. I pictured Philly planting her hands in the soil, and my mum, juice glasses in her hands, confused by what she saw. I was hit by a profound longing to go back to that summer, when I didn't give a thought to my parents ageing or becoming ill, when they remained the still point of my turning world.

I drank the rest of my coffee in one gulp, and threw the paper cup into the bin. I left the cafeteria and made my way to the hospital car park, where my phone started ringing incessantly.

23

You might have an idea of what happened next. You might have seen it on the news:

CILIX CONFIRMS LIQUID OCEAN LIES BENEATH EUROPA'S SURFACE.

ACCORDING TO CILIX FINDINGS, HUMANS COULD LAND ON EUROPA WITHIN THE NEXT DECADE.

NEXT STOP, EUROPA: MASSEY'S SECRET PLAN TO LAUNCH HUMANS FURTHER THAN EVER BEFORE.

In the car park at the hospital, I talked to Louise.

'Hey, Ollie. Mark wants to see you. He's in Germany at the moment, at the ESA headquarters. I'll book you the four p.m. flight.'

'Okay,' I said, hesitantly. 'Could I go tomorrow morning? It's just . . . I've barely seen Philly and Tommy since I came back from the ISS.'

The line went quiet.

'I'm sorry, Ollie. But I think it's urgent.'

I flew to Cologne and was driven to the ESA, where I went straight to Mark's office. Aurélie Gaulthier, the director of the ESA, an elegant woman in her fifties, was standing next to him.

'Ollie,' she said. 'Lovely to see you. I heard your mum was in hospital. I'm sorry.'

'Thank you,' I said. I'm not sure who had told her. 'Lovely to see you too. How was your weekend?'

'Yes, yes,' Mark said, cutting off Aurélie. 'Sorry about your mum, Ollie. Terrible thing. But she's okay, right?' He had a jitteriness to him, which I'd never seen until now.

'Yes,' I said. 'The chemo seems to be working . . .'

'Good,' he said. 'Listen, Ollie, I'm not here to fuck you around. In fact, I think you must already know why you're here, don't you?'

I looked at Aurélie, hoping for some sort of support, but she remained stoic. Yes, I knew. Since when, with what certainty, I've no idea. But as I stood there, Massey sitting behind his glass desk, Aurélie by his side, I had the feeling I was living a scene I'd already lived many times in my head.

'I have some idea,' I said. 'But, please, do go on.'

'Europa,' he said. 'You know we're aiming for a human

mission up there. We began planning ages ago, NovaTech, NASA and the ESA. The most ambitious collaboration for space travel, ever. You remember our conversation last year, right? That was already a decade into the process. But now, with Cilix's findings, we know it's possible. We should be ready to launch in less than three years' time.'

He paused, awaiting my reaction, but so far I had none. 'We've been monitoring you closely. You've had two very successful missions on the ISS and you've excelled in all of your training. You had the highest scores of your cohort in all the aptitude and physical tests. You have twenty years of experience working in hostile environments and with nuclear energy. You're the right age, have the right brain, and the right mindset for the job. And we would like you to be commander.'

His last sentence resonated throughout the room. For what seemed like an eternity, no one spoke.

'Ollie?' Aurélie said carefully. 'We know this is a lot. But would you like to . . . say something, perhaps?'

'I – yes,' I said. 'I'm very flattered, of course. Thank you. I just . . . well, I have some questions.'

'No shit,' Mark said. 'Look, we don't expect you to give an answer right away. You don't have to decide for a couple of months. It's a big decision, of course. Probably the biggest decision of your life.'

'Yes,' I said. 'I'd need to talk about it with Philly. I

mean . . . if I recall correctly, you said the mission would take eight years?'

'Actually, now that we've gathered more data, if we were to avoid the most radioactive areas, both on the journey and on Europa and when taking into account orbital positions . . . it'll take six years to get there, and four years to get back.'

'So, ten years?'

'Ten years.'

I did some quick maths in my head. In two years, Tommy would be five, and I would be forty-two. And ten years from that, we would be fifteen and fifty-two.

'Ollie,' Aurélie said. 'There's something else. The spacecraft is being built out of shielding materials to block harsh radiation, and prevent damage to any human organs. But that means our network won't be able to reach you. You'll be on your own up there. You and the other crew members. But we'll make all kinds of provisions, of course – to ensure you have everything you need and more. And you'll have an A-T on board, too.'

'Okay. I mean, yes, this is . . . this is a bit overwhelming,' I said. 'I have a child, you know. And a wife, and parents . . .'

'We know,' Aurélie said, her tone reassuring. 'As we said, Ollie, we don't expect you to decide right away. There's lots more to discuss, in any case. We just wanted to initiate the conversation, that's all.'

'And who else would go? How many people are we talking?'

'Four,' Mark said. 'You, another of mine, one from the ESA, and one American.'

Another of mine, I thought. But what came out of my mouth was, 'NASA's only sending one?'

'Yes. They're funding a quarter of the mission. They're investing more in the Moon colonies than Europa. Then another quarter ESA, and the rest is us.

'I think NASA's already decided who they'd send,' Aurélie said, skimming through a document. 'A pilot and engineer. Of course, though, as commander, you'd have a say in building the team. I believe you know him . . . Dominic Lewis?'

'Yes, I like Dom,' I said. 'I can't think of a better man for the job.'

'Yeah,' Mark said, standing up. 'That's what NASA said, too. Listen, Ollie, we don't want to bombard you right now. That'd be a waste of breath, for both of us. We know you need time to think. We'll send you a document with all the info, okay? But before you go, let me ask you a question.' He sat at the edge of his desk, his arms folded across his chest. 'Why mechanical engineering? I'm sure a clever guy like you could have made millions in finance by now.'

'Well . . .' I began. 'I suppose I wanted to understand how the structures of the world worked.'

'You could have done physics for that. Or a million other degrees.'

'Yes,' I said, flustered. 'I—'

'I'll tell you my guess, and you tell me if I'm wrong.' He slowed his voice, drawing me in. 'It's because we engineers, we don't just get to know the structures of the world, as you said. No. We get to create them. We get to shape them. We're doers, you and I. Not thinkers. Which is why you should accept. Why you *will* accept.' He pulled away, his face triumphant. 'Because it's in your nature.'

I thought about what my father had made me understand, all those years ago at the Shield: that engineers are makers of dreams.

'Maybe,' I said. 'Maybe you're right. I hadn't really seen it like that. Not in those words, at least. But . . .'

'Ollie,' Mark said. 'We're not talking about a regular mission here. If you do this, and we succeed . . . Forget Armstrong, forget Masuda: you'll be the first man to have travelled that deep into the universe. The first man to walk on Jupiter's moons. And maybe the first man to discover life outside our planet. I mean, we're offering you a pretty unique chance here. We're offering you the key to a mission that basically guarantees you immortality.'

He hopped off his desk. 'But, hey, you have a think. Talk to Philly. Talk to your mum and dad. Louise will be in touch with some more details later today.'

'And please do keep in mind,' Aurélie said, guiding me out of the office, 'that we expect your full discretion. This is all highly confidential, of course.'

I muttered an answer. I shook Mark and Aurélie's hands and left the building, and then I took a taxi back to the airport, alone with my thoughts.

I returned to London that evening, the conversation buzzing in my head.

'Hey,' I told Philly. She was clearing away dinner. I went to hug her, but she ignored my embrace.

'Do you want to put Tommy to sleep?' she said curtly.

'Of course. And afterwards, do you mind if we have a chat?'

'Yeah,' she said, bringing plates into the kitchen. 'I think we should, too.'

Once Tommy was asleep, Philly was waiting for me on the living-room sofa. She had a couple of food stains on her white shirt, and she looked tired. 'You can't go on last-minute trips like that, Ollie.'

'I'm sorry,' I said. 'I tried to tell Louise. I asked if it could wait. But it was urgent.'

'You were supposed to take care of Tommy tonight. I had a conference to attend.'

'I'm sorry. I—'

'Surely whatever it was could have been over the phone.'

'Not really,' I said.

'Well,' she gestured for me to sit next to her, 'do enlighten me.'

I recounted the meeting to her. On the baby monitor we could hear Tommy's snores and the occasional laughter he made while he dreamt, giving our conversation a lulling rhythm.

'Ten years in space? In a tin can?' She sounded more incredulous than annoyed.

'I think so, yes. From their calculations, at least . . .'

'And no contact with Earth that whole time?'

'Yes. Because of the radiation, you know, it's—'

'That is insane, Ollie. That's like . . . a torture experiment.'

'That's one way to see it. But, you know, I think it's doable. It's really not so bad, once you're up there. And it's for a greater cause. Going to Europa . . .'

She let out a sigh and got up, fetched a couple of beers from the kitchen. She opened the bottles, handing one to me. 'Well, it's cool they want you, I guess.' She stayed upright, weighing her words, dubious. 'But it's a no, Ollie. Right? You can't be seriously considering this.'

'No,' I said, fast and defensively. 'Of course it's a no.'

She held her gaze on me a little longer, making sure I meant it. 'Good,' she said, after a few seconds. She brought her beer to her lips, then sat back down. 'I mean, can you imagine? The poor idiot they'll drag up there . . .' And then she laughed, and because I didn't know what else to say, I laughed as well.

We had a pleasant rest of the evening, drinking our beers, her feet resting on my lap. We talked until past midnight, checking in on Tommy occasionally, but at the back of my mind, I couldn't help but replay my conversation with Mark. I suspected he knew I would do so, knew that his words would lodge themselves deep into my mind, that this was exactly what he had wanted, as part of his plan.

PHOENIX MISSION
Commander Oliver Ines's Personal Log

Talos, Day 1712. EVA tomorrow.

We've worked overnight to get the suits ready, checking their batteries and water filter and oxygen levels, the ventilation system etcetera. Lucia has programmed A-T and the walk is relatively straightforward: the deck is only about 500 metres below.

Shane and I are spending the night in the airlock, to get used to the pressure. When I entered he was already there, studying his reflection on his helmet.

'I've gone a bit bald, haven't I?' he said.

'What? No,' I lied. 'I hadn't noticed.'

He turned towards me, deadpan. 'Oh, please.' He observed his reflection again, taken aback. 'I look just like my brother. And he looks just like my dad.'

'How are you feeling?' I asked, trying to change the subject. 'About the EVA, I mean.'

'Fine,' he said, smiling. We were sat on the floor, our backs resting on the wall, next to one another. 'Reminds me of the RAF, being on tour ... the day before sorties. The anticipation and all that. But this is much nicer, actually. Knowing that ...'

'That we're not going to war?'

'Yeah,' he said, grateful that I'd stepped in. 'And it'll be a treat to be outside, for once.' I agreed. 'Do you miss it?' he asked.

'What? Being outside?'

'I don't know. That's a stupid question. Of course you do, right?'

'Yeah. But, honestly ... not as much as I'd imagined I would. The first year, maybe. It was quite tough. I was trying hard not to show it too much. I wanted to be strong, for you three. But now . . . well, I suppose we adapt, don't we?'

'We do,' he said. 'It's not so bad. And we're about halfway, now.'

'Exactly,' I said. 'The next five years, they'll go by so quickly. Before we know it, we'll be back home.'

We stayed quiet for a minute. I was picturing what it would be like to land back on Earth. I think he was doing the same.

'And do you ever get scared?' he asked. 'Of getting home.'

I'd never seen him so vulnerable. For the first time in a while, I watched him attentively. He was forty-six now. His red hair was peppered with grey and, yes, it had receded a bit. His face was a little rougher, with fine lines that hadn't been there a year ago. Yet there was still something undoubtedly youthful about him, and he seemed to me like both a middle-aged man and a lost child seeking reassurance, his long, thin limbs awkward on the floor.

'Sometimes,' I said. 'It'll be a weird adjustment, that's for sure. But it'll be okay.'

'I bloody hope so,' he said, putting his hands behind his head, grinning. 'Otherwise, you'll hear from me. You're the one who recommended me for this, remember?'

We talked for a few minutes longer, and then he went to sleep. I should do the same: we have an early start tomorrow.

24

I've been called many names over the years. I've been called selfish; I've been called selfless; I've been called a hero and a coward. I really didn't think I would accept. I was flattered, yes, and of course I could see the appeal. But I had a wife and a son, a mother who was ill and a job that had already brought me twice into the cosmos. It was enough, I kept telling myself. Surely it was enough.

I don't know the precise moment when that stopped being the case. All the years since, I've tried to come up with an answer that would be satisfying. But just like childhood, or love, or any of those things that can be so clear in one's mind and yet impossible to describe, I suspect that the answer lies partly in feelings: in an urge I had to push the boundaries of what I thought would be available to me. An insatiable curiosity to see how far I could go, how much I could achieve. As the months went by, I began talking to Mark with more certainty, as if I'd already accepted the job.

'We've already interviewed some applicants to fill the

two other positions,' Mark told me. For the first time, he'd invited me on his jet, and we were flying back to London after a quick trip to Germany. We sat across from one another, flutes of champagne on the table between us, which neither of us drank. 'Lucia Bianchi from the ESA has shown interest. She's a physicist. And for the pilot position, we'll go with someone from your cohort. So it's between Ludovic Hugues, or Shane Moore. We're edging towards Ludo. He has marginally higher test scores, for the psychology assessment. Only by a couple of points, though.'

'I've done missions with both of them,' I said. 'Both very able and diligent. They'd both be able to handle it, I believe.' I paused. 'But if I were to choose, I would go with Shane.'

'Yes,' Mark said, watching me closely once more. 'He's your friend, isn't he? You went to Imperial together.'

'He is,' I said. 'But, of course, it's not why I'm saying that. Ludo seemed to me a little nervous during our mission. Whereas Shane really impressed me. He can be ultra-focused, and sharp-minded when needed, while also keeping things light-hearted, and alleviating pressure. Which I think would be important, over such a long period.'

'Fine,' Mark said, 'I guess you're right. And, well, if you *were* to be commander, it would be good to know you're with someone you get on with, wouldn't it?'

'I haven't made up my mind yet, Mark,' I said. 'Lots to think about.'

'Yeah, yeah, I know. You still have a week or two.' He reclined his seat and put on his headphones. 'But keep in mind, we *could* find someone to replace you. The offer won't stand for much longer.'

A stewardess came to escort me to the back of the plane, away from Mark and the champagne flutes, and I understood then that my mind was made up: I wouldn't have mentioned Shane, had it not been. I'm not sure why I had that certainty. Perhaps I knew I wouldn't have suggested him for a mission that I wasn't willing to go through. Or perhaps I knew I would have been too envious to see him up there, while I remained fixed to the ground. Most likely, it was a mixture of both. All I know is that I resolved to talk to Philly once more that evening.

She'd just had a breakthrough at work, discovering new patterns of migration in the *Melitaea didyma*, the spotted fritillary butterfly. She hummed as she heated Tommy's dinner in a saucepan. He was sitting at the table, banging his cutlery, his blond hair, his grey-blue eyes more and more like mine. 'Daddy!' he exclaimed, as I hung my coat. I felt my heart break into tiny pieces.

'Hey, little man,' I said, hugging him, before joining Philly near the stove. It was steaming, the sound of the kitchen fan covering our voices, so that Tommy couldn't hear. 'Hey,' I whispered. 'Can we talk?'

'What's up?' She put the stirring spoon down, wiping her hands.

I clutched the counter. 'It's about the Europa mission.'

'The ten-year one?' she said. 'Did they find someone to replace you?'

She spoke casually, but I could tell by the cautious way she peered at me, that she feared what would come next. She turned her attention to Tommy, facing away.

'No,' I said. 'I just think . . . I think I should do it, Philly. I think I should accept.'

Tommy was getting agitated now. Perhaps he was hungry, or perhaps he had sensed the change in our mood, the tension permeating the air. In an automatic, exhausted motion she filled his bowl with a spoonful of rice and beans and cut-up pieces of chicken.

'Listen, Ollie,' she said, with a calm voice that felt icy. She put the bowl in front of Tommy, who ate gleefully, grains of rice flying everywhere on the table. She picked them up one by one. 'I had a feeling you'd say this. And I can't stop you, if you've already made up your mind. I'm not going to beg you to stay. I won't do that. But just know that if you do this . . . I'm not sure I'll be able to look at you in the same way ever again.'

'It's not necessarily that I want to, Philly,' I jumped in.

'But . . . it's part of my duties. If I don't do this, I feel like I wouldn't have fulfilled—'

'Oh, don't give me that,' she said. 'Your duties? What about us?' She pointed at herself and Tommy, who was crying. She spoke to him in a soothing voice, her face tender once more as she took him in her arms. 'Shh. It's okay, my love.' She carried him to his play mat. I looked on, immobile, the violence of her tone still in my ears. Once Tommy had calmed down, after a minute or two, she came back to the kitchen counter. She spoke in loud whispers, her back to Tommy. '*We're* your duties, Ollie. Fuck NovaTech. Fuck Massey and Europa. I mean, who gives a shit? *We're* here.' She looked at Tommy, who was playing with his figurines, gleeful, and an expression of pity crossed her face. 'There is so much here, on Earth, for you.'

'I know,' I said. I shook my head, desperately trying to find the right words. 'But I'm not just doing it for me, Philly. I'm doing it for Tommy, too. You know better than anyone else that in a few hundred years' time this planet might not even be habitable. We have to start searching elsewhere. The USA's already begun work on our moon.'

'Bullshit,' she said, her voice shaking. 'You're doing it because you want the glory. Because you can't stand anyone else doing it besides you.' On the mat, Tommy became agitated again. 'If our planet is doomed, it's because of people like Mark, and you know it. It's because of men who'd rather invest billions in colonising other planets than saving the one we're on.'

'Look. I didn't say I'd take the job, yet. I'm just . . . I just wanted to discuss the possibility with you. That's all.' I looked at her again, and I saw that beneath her anger, her eyes were wet with tears. Tommy was calling for her, and she went to join him on the mat. I sat at the table alone. Philly and I didn't speak for the rest of the evening. I fashioned a meal out of the leftover rice and chicken, preparing a plate for her, which she ignored. She put Tommy to sleep, and went to bed soon after. I stayed up until late, in the lounge, replaying what she had said in my head. The railway track in the village appeared in my mind. *It's not worth it. It's silly.* I had the strange impression that we were caught in a loop, having a different version of the same argument.

When I did slip under the covers, I did so carefully. 'Philly?' I whispered. She didn't answer, but I sensed that she was still awake. I rolled over to her and put my hand on her shoulder. I felt it shudder.

25

The PHOENIX mission was announced on 12 September 2026, two years before launch. All of a sudden, I was thrust into the spotlight. I did interviews and talks, Q&As and videos, introducing myself, showing the progress of *Talos*, explaining our training. The mission wasn't without criticism. I had to answer tough questions about the risks involved, and the environmental cost of the mission, which brought me back to Professor Whitley's seminar. The benefits of the mission will outweigh its drawbacks, I would say, over and over. Our decision to leave Earth for ten years, too, was not without its controversies. Early on a tweet went viral, attached to a screenshot of me announcing the mission: *Some men would literally rather move to space than go to therapy.*

Not long after I officially joined, Lucia, Dom and Shane came aboard. 'Can you believe it?' Shane said, as we went out for celebratory drinks. 'When we were sitting at that café at Imperial, what, twenty years ago now? If you'd told me back then that this was happening, I'd have told you to fuck off.'

'Me too,' I said. 'How's Liv handling it?'

'Oh, you know,' he shrugged. 'She wasn't pleased, obviously. But she understands. She knew she couldn't stop me. How about Philly? Still angry?'

'That's an understatement,' I said. 'We're not talking much, these days.'

If you closed one eye, perhaps Philly and I could have seemed like any ordinary, happy family. We had mornings and dinners and weekends together. We took Tommy to the park and the zoo, and I took him to school when I wasn't travelling. But in truth, we felt like strangers in our home. Only the day before, as she was coming back from a field trip, I rushed to take her heavy bags. 'Let me,' I said. And then, as I went for the handle our hands brushed, and I felt her fingers and whole body stiffen, as if she had come into contact with something ice-cold. 'I've got it,' she said, avoiding my eyes.

'Sometimes, I think she hates me,' I said matter-of-factly. Shane gave me a look of sympathy.

'She'll come round,' he said. 'She'll understand. Don't worry.'

For two years, we trained almost non-stop: we learnt how to navigate *Talos* inside and out, and how to maintain its reactor. A-T became the fifth member of the team, and we familiarised ourselves with its design. We did team exercises and fire drills, medical and flight training. Lucia, Dom, Shane and I had all done missions together, and we got on brilliantly. It was exhausting, yes, but we were carried through it all by the knowledge that we were prepping for a voyage that broke the boundaries of what had been deemed humanly possible.

Mark checked in on us regularly, his mood jovial as the training progressed. He had a habit of calling us his 'Phoenicians', which irritated Shane to an irrational degree.

'Who does he think he is?' he said, as we were coming back from a mission simulation exercise. 'Why does he act like he's a Roman emperor?'

'He's only trying to be funny,' I said. 'Don't let it get to you. You won't have to see him for ten years soon.'

'That's what I'm most excited about.'

The launch was to take place in French Guiana. About three months before, we had to begin packing our cargo. I was in my bedroom, folding some shirts and trousers, as if planning for a holiday, when Philly came in. She sat on the edge of the bed. She was wearing a green blouse and jeans, and I noticed they were loose on her. 'We need to talk,' she said, her voice strained. I sat next to her. 'When are you leaving for French Guiana?'

'Just over two months,' I said. 'But some of my bags need to get there early.'

'Okay,' she said, staring at an empty spot in front of her. She closed her eyes, pinched her lips together. 'I've tried, Ollie. For Tommy's sake. I've tried for us to be a normal family, the past couple of years. But I can't. I can't do this any longer.' She put her hands over her face, shaking her head. 'Whatever we had, you and I . . . all the things I saw in you . . . it's not there anymore.'

I stayed quiet, focusing on the shirts and trousers neatly folded in their suitcase. I was afraid of what would come out of me if I began speaking.

'I used to love your ambition, and your intelligence. Your calm and your sense of duty and all those qualities that, I'm sure, are why they picked you. But now, when I look at you, all I see is someone who abandoned his wife, child and sick mother.'

I thought of Mum back in the village. Dr Cosler had expressed doubts about whether they would be able to destroy the tumours. 'I understand,' I said, weakly. 'I understand how you would see it this way . . .'

In a month, I would visit the village one last time. 'Didn't I tell you?' Mum said, lightly touching my hair as I struggled to find my words, my whole body shaking. 'Buckets of jam.' She took my hand, giving it a squeeze. I thought about what Philly had said, all those years ago: *We have to let go of our parents a little, while we build our own lives.* Perhaps she was right. Perhaps to achieve our goals it wasn't sacrifice that was required, but rather a letting go. Perhaps our whole lives were just a series of letting go – of certain values and beliefs, of people and memories. We let go of certain things, quietly or with a thud, in the hope of reaching greater, better ones, while the rest wilts away.

Back in London, Philly continued: 'And for *what*? Why are you going? For glory? For science? For the good of humanity? We are right here, Ollie, and we need you. Tommy needs you. And you're leaving us.'

She began to cry, and I wanted to disappear. I wanted to go back to my childhood home, the galaxy wallpaper all over my walls and ceiling, debating whether to reach for Philly's hand.

'I'm sorry, Philly,' I said. 'I really am. I wish . . . I wish it wasn't like this. I wish *I* wasn't like this.'

'You don't *have* to be like this, Ollie.'

'But I do,' I said. 'I know it's hard to understand. Maybe we have fundamentally different points of view. But it's what I'm choosing. I'm choosing to lead this mission, which I think is the most important mission of the century—'

'More important than your wife and child?'

I shook my head, stiffened my posture, embodying my ruthless self. 'I don't like to say it. It pains me. I know you don't think that's the case, but it does. And I also don't want to lie to you. So, yes. I'm doing this mission because I think it's bigger than me, or you, or Tommy. I'm sorry. I understand if you're not able to forgive me.'

I reached for her hand, and with indifference she let me hold it. We sat there in silence, on the edge of the bed, for a minute or an hour, I'm not sure.

'Do you remember the New Forest cicada?' she said, her voice tired and defeated. I pictured Mrs Tan's garden, endless and on a slight slope, roses surrounding us. I heard the cicadas screech, infinite and high-pitched. 'They haven't been spotted since the year 2000,' she said. 'That's just around the time you and I stopped being children. Just around the time we would no longer have been able to hear their sound.' Slowly, she let go of my hand and got up. She turned and held my gaze, taking me in one last time. 'I think this is it, Ollie. We're done.'

PHOENIX MISSION
Commander Oliver Ines's Personal Log

Talos, Day 1714. I'm not sure what to say.

It's been two days, now, since the EVA. It started off well. Shane and I did some final checks, made sure our tethers were correctly attached, and we were off. 'Good luck, guys,' Lucia told us over the radio.

It had been years since we'd done an EVA, and both of us were breathless at what we saw. To our left was Saturn, its rings a brown and gold glow, more resplendent than any photograph could have prepared us for. Right below us was Jupiter, frightening in its vastness, its Great Red Spot surveying us. Though we were still far from it we could make out, clearly, its striped surface of white and orange, of browns and reds. And there, just to its right, barely visible and yet unmistakably there, was Europa.

It brings me some comfort to know that Shane got to see it: our destination, against the backdrop of the universe. A white orb amid darkness.

'Do you see it?' I asked Shane.

'Yes,' he said. 'That bastard.'

'Ollie,' A-T said in my ears. 'Take two steps to your left. Shane, go down by a metre.'

We followed the instructions. Though we were out of practice, it was like riding a bike: our movements became swifter, and in less than half an hour we had reached the main engine deck. I saw the impact of the micrometeorite straight away. A faint dent, about the size of a grapefruit: it was visibly not significant enough to have caused any issues to the reactor or engine inside. Since we had ample time, I considered it wise to carry out some further checks around the surrounding decks, and I asked A-T to guide us.

It was not unpleasant to be out there with Shane in the vastness. Besides A-T's occasional commands, the silence was a welcome respite from

Talos's hum. For a moment, everything felt calm and peaceful.

And then, it happened. We had just reached the other end of the engine deck, so it must have been only a few minutes after we'd seen the impact — ten, perhaps.

'Ollie,' Shane said, a tremor in his voice. I looked back at him. 'Something's wrong.'

That's when I noticed it: a small bubble, an inch or so wide, forming behind his visor, beside his temple.

'Shit,' I said. 'That's okay. Stay calm. We'll get back straight away. A-T, get us back, please.'

By the time I'd finished saying this, the bubble had doubled in size.

I'm not sure what happened. I'm not sure.

Perhaps it was the drink bag, or the cooling system. Whatever it was, it was clear that there was a leak somewhere inside his suit, and that water had begun pooling in his helmet. I saw him trying his best to stay calm, as the bubble grew. We made some progress back towards the ship. Ten, perhaps twenty minutes elapsed. We were only about 400 metres away from the airlock.

'Ollie,' he said, panic in his voice. 'It's starting to blur my vision.'

I heard some static sounds in my ears, followed by silence.

'Shane?' I said. 'Shane?'

He gestured to me that he could no longer hear. The leak must have damaged the radio. And I knew that that meant he could no longer hear A-T either. He did not know which way to go to reach the airlock quickest. He could barely see. I watched in horror, as the bubble got closer to his nose. I moved in his direction and grabbed his arm, dragging him along as fast as I could.

I'm not sure if we realised at the same moment that we would not make it back in time. I'm not sure when I realised. Perhaps it was when I felt his grip loosen, as he began to lose consciousness. Or perhaps I knew before, when I saw him close his eyes and hold his breath as the water reached his nostrils, an expression of calm coming over him. I watched helplessly as he drowned. And even though in the end I could barely see his face through the water, I could have sworn that, in his last moments, his skin was infused with a pale, ice-blue hue.

PART III

26

From backstage, the sound is stifled and faint. She begins in hushed tones, sentences that I cannot make out, until her voice becomes louder and clearer, like someone tuning a radio.

'. . . But now, the PHOENIX team has landed back on Earth!'

The journalists applaud, whistle and cheer. Lucia breathes heavily next to me, apprehension etched on her face. Mark has his hands on our shoulders, grasping them tightly, like a falcon holding its prey.

'It's my great pleasure to introduce to you Aurélie Gaulthier, head of the ESA, Mark Massey director of NovaTech, Dr Lucia Bianchi and Commander Oliver Ines. Please give them a warm round of applause!'

Louise ushers us onto the stage, and for a second the stage lights and the camera flashes blind me. I see Aurélie and Mark waving at the crowd, and I do the same. The presenter motions us forward, and one by one we take our seats.

The presenter continues, 'Before we begin our press

conference, we'd like to observe a minute of silence for Shane Moore. Shane, as you all know, gave his life for the purpose of this mission.' A murmur of approval makes its way across the room. 'For science. For all of us. We will miss him greatly, but find comfort in the fact that he did not die in vain.'

I feel Lucia trying to catch my eye, but I ignore her. As the room falls silent, I gaze up at the audience. There are perhaps a hundred journalists there, mics and cameras and phones pointing at us, their heads down in solemn stillness. On my right, Mark's lips are moving, as if praying. Aurélie's hands are fiddling with the white tablecloth.

'Thank you,' the presenter says, softly. 'I'd like to start with you, Lucia and Oliver. You've been back for a month now – a month you spent in quarantine, and under medical examination. And our hearts are also very much with your NASA colleague Dominic Lewis, who remains under examination. But, for you, now that that's all done, how does it feel to be back?'

At the same time, Lucia and I gesture at one another to take the lead. She insists, and I move closer to my mic.

'Well,' I say, 'obviously, it's a little surreal, and there are a lot of emotions involved. We very much wish Shane could be here with us today, and our thoughts are with his family, and his partner Olivia.' I feel the emotions rushing to my throat. I pause for a second. I hear the click of cameras, and I see flashes. 'So, it's a bittersweet homecoming. And there's a lot we've yet to catch up on. I heard we have people living on our moon now?' Some laughter erupts. I continue my monologue, which I know by heart. 'That's wonderful. I look forward to learning more about all the technological and scientific advances we've made. And, of course, to spend some time with my family and friends, and most of all with my son, whom I've missed so dearly.'

I turn to Lucia, and with a slight nod and a smile I urge her to answer as we'd planned. 'We don't want to linger on that last sentence,' Louise had told us. 'We don't want journalists to jump on your family. But we don't want them to say that you don't care, either. So, mention your son, but let's not dwell on it.'

Lucia clears her throat, and gives a similar answer to mine, finishing with a joke about drinking and eating her weight in wine and pasta, and the audience chuckles. 'That's wonderful. Thank you,' the presenter says. 'Mark, Aurélie, I'd like to turn to you now.' The room shifts to face them. 'This is a huge victory for the space industry, wouldn't you agree? The first humans to land on Europa. Further in space than anyone's ever been.'

'Yes,' Mark says, his posture stiff and straight, his eyes alert. 'Obviously, we regret the loss of Shane. But as you said, he didn't die in vain.' He lifts his chin, looking straight at the reporters, pulling them in like he does so well – they hang on his every word. He points at Lucia and me. 'What these two have achieved – it'll change everything we know about the universe.' He grins at us, as a proud father would. 'It'll change the world.'

'Exactly,' Aurélie continues, her voice higher pitched than usual. 'This was an incredibly ambitious, collaborative enterprise for the ESA, NASA and NovaTech, decades in the making. We're very happy to welcome our heroes home.'

More claps and cheers and whistles, so many sounds and so many faces, the flashes blinding me again. Yet I notice some journalists abstaining, simply glaring at us with mistrust.

'Well said indeed,' the presenter says. She turns to face the audience. 'And now, we'll take some questions. Yes, you?' A journalist on the front row stands up.

'Hi there,' he says. His voice sounds younger than I expected. 'Joe Wood, *The Economist*. I think I speak for everyone when I say we want to know: are there aliens out there?' The audience laughs again. With a tilt of the chin, Mark prods me to answer.

'Well,' I say, 'we're still in the process of analysing all of the samples we brought back. It'll take some time for us to answer that question with any certainty.' I turn to Aurélie and Mark for support. 'And it's important to note that if there is life on Europa, it'll be in a shape vastly different from life on Earth, almost unrecognisably so.' I give a faint smile. 'But what I will say is that, from the results we've had so far, there's substantial evidence that Europa holds all the required chemical elements for life to exist and evolve there.' I look to my right. Mark and Aurélie nod approvingly. The presenter points to another journalist.

'Juliette Perrin, AFP. There are a lot of unanswered questions about Shane Moore's passing. Could you tell us what happened, exactly?'

Aurélie begins to speak, but Mark cuts her off. 'We're conducting a full investigation into Mr Moore's tragic death. We're as determined as you are to know exactly what happened.' He becomes pensive, as if weighing each of his words with the utmost care – though this too is rehearsed. 'From our initial inquiry, we didn't find any sort of defect in his suit that might have contributed to the accident.' I can sense Lucia's tension: she's angry. 'But you have to remember that our astronauts were working in extremely hostile environments, for an extended period of time,' Mark continues. 'Any small human error could have proven fatal. And I want to take a moment here to give our thanks to Ollie, who put himself in great danger to bring Shane's body back to *Talos* and return him to Earth.'

I watch the sea of faces turn towards me, scrutinising my every expression. There are more clicks and more flashes – but in my head I'm back in the cosmos, its darkness so deep that everything here feels too bright in comparison. I see Shane closing his eyes and holding his breath, as he drowned in his suit. I feel the silence that followed, his body floating limply, hanging loose from his tethers. And then, regaining my awareness as my new goal became clear, like a beacon in the mist. My hand reaching for his arm, and it not reaching in return. Manoeuvring his unwieldy body to *Talos*, as A-T signalled my depleting oxygen.

'Ollie, that was a very brave thing you did,' Mark continues. 'Thank you.'

More applause, this time lighter. The presenter has already called for another question. But I stay with Shane for an instant longer, picturing Lucia's face as I entered the airlock again.

'Mike Tran, *Washington Post*. Could you tell us more about Dominic Lewis's condition? Is he okay?'

'Yes,' Aurélie jumps in. 'He'll be fine. He's getting all the care he needs to make a full recovery. During a ten-year mission, the odds of one of our astronauts getting ill was not insubstantial.'

'So, he *is* ill?'

'Medical examinations have shown signs of an illness, yes. I'm afraid I cannot disclose more at this time – Mr Lewis would like to speak to his family first. But he's okay.' Aurélie waves a hand at the presenter.

'Thank you. Next question, please.'

'Emma Brandt, DPA. This is a question for Oliver Ines.' I jerk to attention. 'Commander Ines, you were the only one on the team to have a child. I wonder, how did you rationalise leaving him, as well as your wife, for this mission? And do you have any remorse?'

'I'm not sure this question is directly relevant to the mission . . .' the presenter says, glancing at Louise, hiding backstage.

In truth, I'm relieved to hear it: I had been waiting for it. I can feel everyone's eyes on me, some curious and prying, others disdainful. I was expecting shame, but it's not exactly the emotion I feel. Instead, I feel a slowness in my body, a numbness in the way I approach the mic.

'It's okay. I can answer,' I say. I collect my thoughts. 'It was a very tough decision. The most difficult one I'll probably ever have to make. And, in a way, it was an impossible choice. Not to see my family for ten years. To miss my son's childhood and all the milestones that come with it. I suppose that's something I'll always regret, to some extent.' In the crowd, I hear someone cough. 'It's not a choice I expect everybody to understand. But just because I feel regret doesn't mean I would change anything.' I pause, catching my breath. 'At the end of the day, I chose the path that, I believed, could provide a better future for him. One that holds fewer mysteries, and a better understanding of our place in the universe. A future my son can be proud of – and proud that his dad played a part in creating it.'

I catch Louise breathing a sigh of relief – and in my head, I hear Philly's voice: *Bullshit.*

'Have you seen your son, yet?' the journalist continues.

'Well, No . . .' I say. 'I've been in quarantine and . . .'

'When will you see him and your wife? Commander Ines, where is your son?' Hints of a commotion break in the room, more flashes, more whispers.

'That's enough for now, thank you,' the presenter says. The room calms down.

There are more questions, about taxpayers' money and CO_2 emissions, hoax allegations and radiation. But there's only one that I hear, over and over again.

'Commander Ines, where is your son?'

———

'Fucking hell, that was brutal,' Mark says. He opens his bottle of sparkling water, as Lucia glowers at him. 'Ah, well, wouldn't have expected anything less. You two did very well.'

Louise ushers us out of the backstage area. Someone asks for my autograph, someone else for a picture, and I oblige. We arrive at a corridor. Aurélie stays behind, answering more questions from journalists.

'So that's it?' Lucia asks, rushing up to Mark. 'We're just going to lie to everyone?'

I restrain my pace, reluctant to get involved. In front of

me, Mark shushes Lucia. 'You can't go around shouting things like that. Here, get in.'

We ride the lift up to his office, the same office I had stood in more than a decade ago, when he offered me the commands of *Talos*. The room is more cluttered. There are rows of awards on the shelves, some paintings framed in gold – a Warhol, a Picasso, which I can only assume are real. His glass desk has been replaced by a sleek silver one. He takes a seat and motions for us to do the same, but Lucia remains standing. Through the window behind his desk, I can see the Shard, the London Eye and Big Ben.

'So, what is it you want to say?' he asks Lucia.

'You know very well that Shane didn't die because of human error. You know Dom didn't get ill because of the passage of time—'

'I know that Shane tended to be overly confident in his actions, and that he had a reckless streak.' He gestures my way, then to himself. 'Which is why *we* had initially suggested Ludo.' My eyes stay fixed on the silver desk. 'But it doesn't matter,' he continues. 'We knew that the odds of one of you getting seriously ill during the journey were about one in two. I mean, for goodness' sake, why did you think your contracts were so long? You knew the risks.'

'You sent us up there with designer suits in a cheap spacecraft,' Lucia says. Her voice is quiet, almost a whisper, and furious. 'And with a fucking robot. But it was all for show, wasn't it? The suits were poorly designed, and the radiation-shielding failed us. Did you really test them before sending us up there like guinea pigs? How could that happen to Shane? How could it happen to Dom, if you had? It's a miracle any of us are still alive.'

'Trust me,' he says, rising slowly to his feet, and I grasp how he became the most powerful man in the world. There is menace in his tone, which he had only hinted at before. It reminds me of a viper, quiet yet deadly. Lucia takes a step back. 'If the technology didn't work, you *would* be dead. But you're not, are you? You're here. Shane's death was a tragic accident, and Dom's illness a very sad occurrence.' He sits down again and blinks, taking a second to compose himself. I see his muscles relaxing, and suddenly all the menace is gone, his tone conciliatory. 'Now, you can either agree with that, or take it up with HR.'

The three of us come to a standstill. Lucia turns towards me. 'Ollie,' she says, with threatening calm, 'are you going to say anything?'

But I don't see the point. Both are right, and both are wrong. A hollowness has come over my whole being. I had recommended Shane over Ludo. The suit should not have leaked. Dom's results showed high levels of radiation exposure, but they could have been from a previous mission he had done. Or perhaps, like Shane's, his suit had had a defect that hadn't shielded him as ours had.

Mark and Lucia wait for an answer. On Mark's desk is a beautiful antique magnifying glass, with an ivory handle. I detach myself from it and meet Lucia's eyes. They're filled with hate.

'Coward,' she whispers. She storms out of the door.

Mark takes a long breath, halfway between relief and exasperation. 'Well, that's that,' he says, stretching his arms. He observes me for a moment. 'For God's sake, Ollie, say something. You look miserable.' I notice the waxiness of his skin, its tightness, how ageing seems to have escaped him.

'How's Dom doing?' I ask.

Mark shakes his head, standing up. 'Not good. Christ, they showed me the scans . . . It's spread all over his body. They don't know if he'll make it to the end of the year.'

I picture Dom's mum and dad in their St. Louis Cardinals caps, the photograph of them that he carried on *Talos*, tucked between the pages of his Bible. I see him playing guitar to entertain us, his fingers caressing the strings. I think of him pondering the universe through the control deck, and finding in it something divine. 'We won't give the press an update, though,' Mark continues. 'No. We'll wait for it to die out – sorry, bad choice of words. We'll wait for things to calm down, and then when the time comes, we'll make a press release about his passing.'

'That's pretty cold, Mark,' I say. I hadn't remembered

Mark like this. I had remembered him as brusque and blunt, yes, but not cruel. But there is a more vicious element to his demeanour that matches his ascendancy over the world.

'Yes, it is,' Mark says. 'But that's just how it has to be. One death is a tragic accident in a heroic mission. But two deaths? That's two lives wasted on a reckless assignment. And surely you know we can't have that.'

'I saw it. *Pegasus*. We all did.'

'I know,' he says. 'You don't think I read your log entries? I mean, Jesus, Ollie. Really? Overriding the autopilot? What the hell were you thinking? You're lucky that this can't get out. I'd have loved nothing more than to make you the scapegoat for all this crap.' He waves his hands frantically around his office. For the first time, I feel like he's not fully in control of himself. 'But no. We can't be reminding people of HEPHA, not right now. You never saw anything. You went straight to Europa.'

'But it was the same story, wasn't it? On the wreckage. We could tell that an explosion had happened. We couldn't really see. We were still far away. But . . . I looked at its design. And I compared it to the wreckage. It was the reactor, wasn't it? The reactor malfunctioned. Same story as with *Challenger*. Same with us. There was a fault with the equipment, and it killed them.'

'How the fuck should I know? And you. You know nothing. You decided to go on your little side adventure, and what good did that do? You think that micrometeorite would have hit you if you hadn't overridden the autopilot? You think you'd have had to go on that EVA with Shane, if you hadn't been such an idiot?' He walks to his window and surveys the city below him, leaning against the glass.

I let his words pass through me. They're nothing that I haven't been telling myself for the past five years. 'You know,' I say, 'when I was up there, I reflected on what you told me. About how we became engineers, so that we could shape the structures of the world.'

'Yeah,' he says, contemptuous. 'Did you realise I was right?'

'Maybe you are,' I say. 'But the difference between you and I is that you wish to shape them to control them. To control everything.' His silence tells me he is listening. 'I don't think that's true of me. I wanted to shape them because I like to actualise potential. Because I wanted to see how many dreams, how many possibilities could become realities.'

He glares at me, before scoffing and shaking his head. 'What happened up there, seriously? Have you all become lunatics?'

'What happens next?' I ask, ignoring him.

He turns around, laughing. 'What do you mean, what happens next? You're done. You're a hero. Catch up on ten years' worth of film and TV. See your family and friends.

Get an agent and a book deal. Go to a bar, get drunk, meet some girls. They'll be throwing themselves at you.'

'But for the mission,' I say. 'What happens next, to Europa?'

'Don't play dumb. You know how it goes. You see what's happening on the Moon and on Mars. First we observe, then we send probes, then you. And then we mine.' I see his mind spinning with the prospect of all of the opportunities I've opened up to him. 'Some of those ice samples you brought back show the presence of scandium. We could build lighter aircraft with that. And helium-3 – we could use that as fuel in the nuclear reactor.' I catch a flash of the science geek I imagined he had once been. 'Of course, if there is indeed life, we'll deal with that, too.'

I think about Lea Mann: *Whatever you do, you'll be a pawn.* 'You'll use what we mined to advance our technologies,' I say. 'And then you'll repeat the process.'

'Exactly. We'll go deeper and deeper into the universe.' He looks down at the city again, as if it were his playground. And I can see that in his mind, this meeting, this whole mission, is already far behind him. 'That's just what we do.' He advances towards the door and smiles as he opens it, a cue for me to leave. 'But don't worry. No one remembers the name of the ones who come after. Only the first. Armstrong, Masuda, Ines . . . They will only remember you.'

PHOENIX MISSION
Commander Oliver Ines's Personal Log

Day 2190. D-Day.

Talos landed on the ice with a thud. After some back and forth, we agreed that Dom would come out with us, despite his pain, for a short while – it would have been cruel to prevent him.

We put on our suits. I helped Dom with his, and I was alarmed to see how thin he had become. He caught me glancing at his ribs, worry etched on my face. He grabbed my hand, holding it as tight as he could, a shake in his palm. 'It's okay,' he said, in his calm voice. 'Today . . . this is your moment. This is what you've been working towards your whole life. Enjoy it.'

I told him thank you with a nod, without quite the courage to meet his eyes. I finished helping him with his suit. I noticed Lucia struggling to fasten her helmet, and I gave her a hand. 'Thanks,' she said. 'I don't know why I'm so nervous.'

After some final checks, I reached for the handle of the airlock. 'Ready?' I asked.

It's only now that I realise, that I was so enthralled by the moon, so overwhelmed, that I failed to utter proper landing words. Or perhaps unconsciously, I did not wish to say them without Shane there to tease me afterwards. No doubt I will have to come up with some retrospectively. But for now, what I will say is, that it was indeed very strange, after six years, to arrive at our destination.

I took the first step on Europa's icy crust. As always when I left the craft, the silence engulfed me. I leapt high, and from up there I saw its smooth surface, bright and resplendent. I saw the reddish-brown cracks that criss-crossed it, which I had spent so much time observing back home.

As I began to fall back down gently, I had the odd sensation that I was stumbling onto a dream. I cannot quite explain the feeling that emanated from the moon and from me. All my movements felt surreal, as if they were delayed - as if I was controlling my body remotely, both in charge of and removed from it. And I felt that at any moment, the ice might shatter beneath my feet, like glass, and I might disappear completely.

I gave Dom and Lucia the all-clear. They emerged slowly, unsure, with A-T behind them, like bears coming out of hibernation. None of us said anything. Perhaps they felt similarly to me: that by speaking we risked breaking the spell, and all of this would reveal itself as unreal. Lucia bent down, and with the tip of her gloves, caressed the surface. Her fingers left no trace on the ice.

After some trial and error, we found different ways to move about: I favoured a kangaroo-like hop, while Lucia and Dom took giant leaps. The reality of the situation settled in, and a sense of relief permeated us: we had made it, finally. We gave each other hugs, no easy feat with our suits and the gravity. I know that all three of us were thinking of Shane, and that we felt his presence.

We got to work. A-T started drilling into the ice, which took a while: it did not break easily, and when it did it was only in minuscule fragments, like snowflakes. Lucia made use of the spectrometer, and did some tests on the air and ground. Dom took photographs, and after ten minutes or so retreated to *Talos*. I caught him taking one last long glimpse at the planet, taking in all of its last details – its diamond-like glow, its smoothness and bareness and – how else to put it? – its perfection.

As A-T began to make good progress on the drilling, and we had a reasonable number of samples, a strong sensation of tiredness crept in me. I turned to Lucia, who was swaying lightly from side to side, her hand resting on top of her helmet. 'Lucia,' I said. 'Are you okay?'

'Yes,' she said. 'Just a bit dizzy.'

'We should go soon.' I avoided telling her that I felt the same. 'We can't stay out for much longer.'

Within a short time – fifteen minutes or so, we'd packed away the samples, and made our way back to *Talos*.

Perhaps it was the atmosphere, or exhaustion after a day high in emotions and labour – but on top of the dizziness, I began to feel feverish. That was when things began to blur.

Though I don't remember how, I removed my suit, and got out of the airlock. I knew what I had to do next. I took the ice samples that A-T had so carefully gathered. I made my way to the cold room, more like a large cupboard, and I began to feel dread.

We had placed him in his sleeping bag so that he wasn't visible as I came in. Yet as I entered the room, and I saw the bag strapped to the wall, I felt certain I saw him clear as day, his body limp and lifeless, his face pale blue. I know I sound mad, but as I placed the samples in the containers behind him, I heard his voice.

'You could stay here, you know,' Shane said.

I placed my hand on the handrail to my right. The cold seeped into my fingers, tingling like pins and needles. The air prickled my eyes, and imbued the room with a soft haze.

I tried to silence the voice as best I could, yet it continued.

'There's nothing left for you down there, is there? Your mum is dead. Your wife hates you. So does your son. Why don't you stay here?'

'You're not real,' I said. 'Shane would never say that.'

'Maybe he would,' he said. 'Maybe he would say that, after what you did to him.'

I believe that I screamed, though again it might have been inside my head. I stumbled out of the room. I tried to close the door behind me, but the handle wouldn't budge. I called for help.

'Ollie?' Lucia said. 'Here, let me.' With a swift movement, she closed the door.

'Thank you,' I said.

'You don't look well, Ollie.'

'No,' I said. 'I think ... I think I'm going to lie down for a moment. Can you and A-T manage the rest?'

Without waiting for her answer, I left the room.

27

At first sight, the village is the same. There is still the Shield and the church and the postman doing his rounds, the railway track and the hill on the eastern side. Yet when I look closely, holding the two images side to side, I notice the changes. The tea shop has shut down and there are smart locks on the front doors of some houses, including on Mr and Mrs Burns's. Dad tells me they've moved to a retirement home, and that it's now a holiday rental. When I go for a walk to the other side of the village, I see a gap in the scenery that the old sycamore used to fill, its summer leaves once a vibrant green.

I go into my childhood bedroom. My superhero figurines are neatly sat on my bookshelf, my books in a cardboard box by my bed. The wallpaper is still there, its edges peeling away. I turn off the light and draw the curtains, and I see that the planets and the stars no longer glow in the dark.

I make dinner. My movements are shaky and it takes me a while to chop the onion and peel the potatoes. The knife, the peeler, everything is heavy in my hands, tiring me. Perhaps it's being back here or my clumsy movements, but I feel like a child again. In the room next door Dad is watching a TV show I'm unfamiliar with while half-asleep, his hand resting on the remote. I place the vegetables in the oven, the sausages on top. While we wait, I join him in the lounge.

'What are you watching?' I ask.

'Oh,' he says. 'You wouldn't know it, huh? It's this detective show I've been enjoying. It's wrapping up, now.'

Once the credits roll, he turns off the telly. Outside it's still daylight, and we can hear children playing in the street. He pulls a bottle of old whisky from the cabinet. 'Want a drink?'

'No, thanks,' I say. 'I'm not used to alcohol yet. Got pretty ill the other day, after a couple of beers.'

He pours himself a small glass and goes to get ice from the freezer.

'That's new, isn't it? The whisky, I mean. I've never seen you drink it.'

'Yes. I suppose it's new for you. But it's been a few years now. I started after your mum died.' He brings the glass to his mouth, and my heart sinks. 'It gave me something to do, in the evenings.'

He takes a sip, a droplet falling on his beard, which he doesn't notice. He puts the glass down. His eyes remain on the telly's black screen, in which we can see our reflections. When I catch sight of mine, I realise I resemble my dad more than I resemble myself.

'I'm sorry,' I say, on an impulse. 'I'm sorry I wasn't there when Mum died.'

His face lifts in surprise, as if for a moment he'd forgotten I was there.

'Oh, well . . . It's been almost seven years now.' He stares at his glass. 'I miss her every day. But we find ways, don't we? We find ways to keep going.'

I don't ask if it was quick and easy, or if death tugged at her, slowly and painfully. Perhaps later I will ask. Perhaps later I will rouse the courage, and ask my dad to recount to me the most painful days of his life. I'd spent so much time worrying about coming back to a world without my mother that I forgot to worry about coming back to a world in which my father was alone and in his eighties, his lust for life vanished – a stranger so familiar.

The back of the winged armchair dwarfs him, as if he might vanish between its cushions. I picture him on the same chair forty-odd years ago, joining my mum to watch the nine o'clock news once he'd finished the washing-up. He'd go and sit in the armchair, and I'd find myself imitating his posture, pulling my chest forward, straightening my back and my shoulders.

'Do you remember your old friend, Jimmy?'

'Jimmy Lovett?' I ask. I haven't heard his name in over a decade.

'Yes, that's right. Him and his wife, they took over the family farm, around the time you left. They've managed to expand it by quite a bit, actually. They've been very kind to me, over the years. Used to bring me meals when your mum was in hospital. And even now, sometimes, Jimmy will drop by for a chat, with some fresh eggs or some vegetables.'

'So . . .' I say, 'he's doing okay, then?'

'Oh, better than that, I'd say. Got two nice kids as well. Two boys. The eldest's off to uni now. Yes, I'd say he's doing quite alright.'

I wonder if they're friends with Tommy, but I don't ask. Instead, I just say, 'That's good. I'm happy for him.' And as the words leave me, I realise I mean them.

We talk some more. He asks me how we occupied ourselves up there, and I tell him about the treadmill, the cleaning and the banter, the card games and books and music. I consider telling him about Dom's guitar, but I find that just thinking of it makes my throat tight. He asks me what it felt like, seeing Earth from up there, and landing on a moon, a planet that is not yours. And I say, with sincerity, that it was both extraordinary and lonely – but I leave it at that. I don't add that as I stepped onto

Europa I wasn't filled with elation, or an exhilarating sense of accomplishment. There were hints of it, perhaps, but mostly, there was that strange feeling of loneliness and detachment – as if I didn't quite belong to either place anymore. And that when I heard Shane's voice, in the cold storage room, telling me I could stay on Europa, for a brief and mad second, I was tempted.

In turn, I ask him more questions about the village. He tells me there is still Morris dancing in the spring at the Shield, that children continue to smoke their first cigarettes on the bench near the church. That even though Joe Harding's fields have gone, the smell of manure lingers, as if it has merged with the air. And as he tells me those details he begins to drift somewhere far away, and the only sound that remains are the ice cubes tinkling in his half-empty glass.

The beeper goes off, making me jump, and I go to check the food.

'Five more minutes,' I say, sitting back down.

He swirls his drink around. 'So,' he says, finally. 'Any news from Philly, then?'

'Yes,' I say. 'We've emailed. I'm meeting her next week. She and Tommy are away for the summer break.'

'That's good,' Dad says. 'Very good. We've kept in touch. Quite regularly, in fact. Tommy's turning into a fine young man, I must say. She's done a wonderful job raising him.'

That last sentence stings, but I let it pass. 'I'm sure she has,' I say. I hesitate. 'What's he like?'

Dad smiles. 'You'll see soon enough. But what I will say is, the apple doesn't fall far from the tree.'

'You mean he's like Philly? Or me?'

'A bit of both.' For a moment, he seems unsure of himself. He strokes his beard absently. 'But . . . when I spent time with him, and you were gone, it made things a bit more bearable. It was like having you back as a child, in a way. A chance to make things right, I suppose.'

'What do you mean?' I ask. 'Make things right how?'

He sighs. 'Well . . . I wish I'd been a bit more like I am with him, with you.' His eyebrows furrow. 'I feel like I was a bit tough on you sometimes. Oh, not terrible, I know. You should have seen how I was raised. But I suppose I could have shown you a bit more . . . What was it your mum would always tell me? Tenderness. Yes, that's right.' He lets out a small laugh. 'She was always much better at that, wasn't she? Not really my area. I was always the quiet one, between us two.'

'It's okay, Dad,' I say. I feel my eyes welling up. 'You were great. You did a good job, honestly.'

'Well, I wasn't the worst. But I've had a lot of time to think, lately. And I sometimes worry that, maybe, if I'd been different somehow, when you were younger, maybe you would have stayed.'

'No,' I say. 'No, really, Dad, it wasn't anything like that. It wasn't anything to do with you. It was just something I had to do. Something I felt I had to do.'

He lets out a sigh, relieved. 'That's good to hear,' he says. 'Here, I want to show you something.' He goes to the cupboard behind him, and takes out a photo album, thick and well-loved.

'I've been collecting articles about you over the years. I began before you left. I never told you but, well, here it is. I thought you might like to see it.' He hands me the album. *Oliver Ines*, it says on the cover, and underneath, my official NovaTech astronaut photo, taken when I'd first joined. I look very young.

'Thank you,' I say. 'I had no idea you had this.'

I open it, and there are articles about my first trip to the ISS, and my second. There are photos of me and the PHOENIX crew in our NovaTech uniforms, smiling broadly in front of *Talos*. I turn the pages, and I come across a photo of Shane and Dom, happy as can be, testing out the pilot system, me observing them from behind. On the final page, there's a *Times* article, headline: TRIUMPHANT RETURN HOME FOR THE PHOENIX CREW – and just beneath it, a photo of me as I emerged from *Talos* in the middle of the ocean, pale and dazed, carried by two men, not yet reacquainted with gravity.

'Kept me busy,' Dad says, looking at the album over my

shoulder. Outside, I hear parents calling their children home, as the sunlight begins to fade. The smells of grilling meat and garlic reach the living room.

'Thank you, Dad,' I say, as I close the album with care. 'I think the food's ready, now.'

I help him up, and we make our way to the kitchen, his hand on my arm.

28

The train's air-conditioning is broken and it's hot and overcrowded. There are passengers standing all throughout the carriage. Finally, I think I understand what people mean, when they ask me if I ever feel claustrophobic. I keep my head turned to the window and I watch the scenery pass, fields of wheat and sunflowers, horses feasting on hay. As we arrive in Margate, for the first time in ten years I see the sea. I gape at it with longing, when I hear someone shouting.

'Hey! Aren't you that astronaut?'

Three schoolboys, sat further down in the carriage, approach me.

'Yes,' I say, producing a smile. I notice one of them is filming me. He must be around sixteen, Tommy's age. 'Yes, I am. Pleasure to meet you all.'

'So, what's space like, then?' Around the carriage, people are beginning to turn, whispering to one another.

'Well,' I say, 'It's—'

'Did you meet any aliens?' The three of them burst out laughing.

I keep my composure. We arrive at a station – not mine, but I pretend otherwise. 'Afraid that's my stop, lads,' I say as I stand up, my smile clinging on. 'I'll have to tell you another time.' I get off the carriage, and discreetly climb into a different one at the other end of the train.

Liv's hair has gone white. Her face has wrinkles where before there was smoothness, and the hollows under her eyes have widened. 'Come in,' she says. 'Thanks for coming all the way here.'

'Of course,' I say. 'Lovely place you've got.'

'Thank you. I moved here not long after you left, actually. I craved the fresh air of the sea.'

Her flat is cramped and overlooks the shore, seagulls flying high above the sea. I notice dishes piled up in the sink, dust on the windowsill, and a faint stale smell. I remember that, while I've had five years to grieve Shane, she's had only a month.

'You want coffee? Tea?'

'Coffee would be great, thank you. Black is fine.'

She pours ground beans into the French press. I sit down on the sofa. On the side-table next to me, there's a framed photo of her and Shane in their twenties. They're holding each other at the waist, on top of a mountain, wide grins filling their faces. Shane is staring back at me, and I shudder.

'Oh, that was in Wales,' says Liv, handing me my coffee. 'When we climbed Snowdon. Lovely day, that was.' She sits down across from me, and I put the photo back.

'So. I think we both know what we'll end up talking about, don't we?' she says, in a quiet, gentle manner that unsettles me. 'So, how about we cut the bit where we pretend to make small-talk and go straight to it, if you don't mind?'

'Yes,' I say. 'That's fine by me.'

'Was it painful?'

'No. He wouldn't have realised what was happening to him.'

'Good,' she says. 'That's good.'

'Yes. It happened in an instant.' I take notice of how easily the lies come. 'He was cracking jokes only a few minutes before it happened.'

'That's good. I suppose I should thank you. For bringing him back.'

'There's nothing to thank me for.' I hesitate, the porcelain cup fragile in my hands. I'm scared to break it. 'I'm sorry, Liv. I really am. I wish none of it had ever happened.'

She smiles down at the picture frame. I feel her pondering whatever she's about to say. 'You know, Ollie, I never really liked you.'

I almost choke on my coffee, which burns my throat. 'Oh. Is that so?' I don't know what else to say.

'Yes. I was never quite sure what Shane found in you. Or Philly, for that matter. You always struck me as cold. Or uninterested. I mean, do you even know what I do for a living?'

'I . . . well . . . Not really.'

'I'm a teacher, Ollie.'

'Oh,' I say. An image of my mum, in front of her classroom, pops into my head. 'That's wonderful.'

'Yes. I teach at the senior school just down the road. Used to teach at a school not that far from you back in Surrey.'

'That's great,' I say. 'I'm sorry. I'm sorry I didn't know.'

'It's okay,' she says. 'I guess my point is, that we never really bonded, did we? But we had Shane in common. And, Ollie, your friendship – it made him so happy. He was so happy when you both joined NovaTech. And he was so happy when you chose him for the mission.' Although I listen for it, I do not hear accusation in her tone.

'Thank you for saying that,' I say. On her wall, I recognise Shane's painting, the one he had shown me on his phone. Its energy is more violent than I remember.

'It was hard, of course. I was furious with you for a while. Never really with him. We had some back and forth, obviously. But who was I to stop him? We didn't have children, at least.' She peeks in my direction, and then she continues: 'The way I ended up seeing it was that it was a part of our story. I mean, we were together for twenty years before he left. What was ten years apart, in the grand scheme of things? Only a chapter, for us.'

'That's a lovely way to see it. That's—'

'And what about up there?' she adds. 'Was he happy?'

Back on *Talos* I see Shane at the kitchen table, head resting on his palm, porridge floating above his spoon. I picture him staring at the dwindling Earth from the porthole, engraving her in his mind, and I feel myself twisting on the sofa.

I don't tell Liv that Shane had doubts about the mission: I don't see the point in upsetting her. I don't tell her about his bouts of depression, when *Talos* would become blue and morose as a result. Instead, I continue making up a story.

'He was,' I say. 'I mean, of course, like all of us, he missed Earth. And he missed you.' I look out to the sea. 'But he was the life of the ship. He made us laugh so much.'

'I miss his stupid jokes.'

'Me too,' I say. We sit quietly for a minute. I wait to see if she'll ask me more questions, but she seems to have had enough. 'Well,' I say, after I've finished my coffee, 'I don't want to keep you. I'll get going, I think.'

She doesn't protest, and we stand up. I bring my mug to the kitchen sink, placing it on a pile of grease-stained plates.

'Thank you again for coming,' she says. 'I'll be in touch soon, anyway. With the solicitor.'

I must make an odd face because she adds, 'Don't worry. Nothing bad. Shane left you some money in his will. Two hundred pounds, to be precise.'

She waits for my response, inquisitively. It takes me a second, but then I understand. 'Oh, yes,' I say. 'I think I know what that's for. It was a joke. He lost a bet we'd made, a long time ago.'

'I see,' she says. 'I thought it would be something like that.'

'Liv,' I say. 'I don't want that money.'

'I don't want it either,' she says, and for the first time in our conversation, I hear contempt. She walks me to the door. 'It's yours. Do whatever you want with it. Or ask his brothers, if you wish. It's been hard for them, losing their baby brother.'

'Right,' I say. 'Of course.'

She beams, more to herself than me. 'Commander Oliver Ines,' she says. 'The hero, the star.'

I turn around, puzzled.

'That's what you'll be from now on, isn't it? A national hero.' Her smile is still there, disturbing me. 'But we don't really feature in your story, do we? Shane's brothers and me. Not even Shane, not really. He won't be a part of the story of Oliver Ines. Or if he is, he'll be the sidekick, right? The Robin to your Batman.'

I try to say something, anything, but I've become mute. She sniggers, as if she had been expecting this. She opens the door briskly, and when I remain standing there she puts her hand on my shoulder amiably but firmly. 'Goodbye, Ollie,' she says, ushering me out.

PHOENIX MISSION
Commander Oliver Ines's Personal Log

Talos, Day 3550. We're beginning to see the light at the end of the tunnel, but morale is low.

Dom continues to do his mandatory treadmill time, and some jobs around *Talos*, but spends most of his day in his sleeping bag. He never complains, but I catch him grimacing in pain when he thinks I'm not looking, or clutching his stomach, and each time it distresses me. We ran out of painkillers a while ago, now.

Lucia grows quieter. I suspect she will be glad to have someone else for company once we land. She's called Mark and Aurélie by some colourful names. Though, of course, it's only natural that as years went by, certain resentments would arise. Yesterday, she cornered me as I made my lunch (our last pouch of macaroni and cheese).

'Ollie, we need to talk,' she said. I signalled that I was listening.

'One hundred days before landing,' she said. 'And our two pilots are out of action.'

'Dom is still here ...' I began, but I stopped when I saw how she looked at me: with incredulity and anger.

'We've been trained for landing,' I said instead. 'It'll be fine.'

'Really? You remember your training from ten years ago? And you trust those weird VR machines we've been using on board?'

'Yes, I do, actually.' She rolled her eyes dramatically. 'I know it's not ideal. But it is what it is. The autopilot and A-T should be able to do most of the work. And then, when it comes to the more detailed manoeuvring ... well, as I've said, we've been trained for it. We've been training all these years, on those weird VR machines, as you call them.'

As she embarked on another rant about NovaTech, the mission and Massey, I tried to recall said training – the difficulty of entering Earth's orbit at just the right angle, so that *Talos* didn't burn to a crisp or bounce back into the void – the swift, fast and precise motions needed.

It will be a delicate matter, undoubtedly – one that will require our utmost concentration and agility. All skills that Shane and Dom had, but that, thankfully, I've also demonstrated in previous missions, and on the VR simulations. I'm fairly confident we'll manage. And, after all, what choice do we have? Either we try, or we perish. And we have done too much – we have sacrificed too much – not to try.

29

I wonder if I should stop at the bakery first. In the shop window there are lemon pies and strawberry tarts, chocolate cakes and Paris-Brests. I haven't had any pastries since coming back: I find that even fruit is too sweet for me.

Perhaps I should get him a present, too. Though I'm not sure what sixteen-year-olds like, these days. In any case, she told me it would just be her today – and though it hurts to admit it, when she told me I breathed a sigh of relief.

I go to Gypsy Hill. I've never been to this part of London before, and as I walk I can't help but picture my life here, had I stayed. There's a farmers' market with fresh sourdough bread, a fishmonger and a butcher. There's a bookshop and coffee shops and plant shops, young families with pushchairs going towards the park, groups of friends gathered in pubs.

As I ring the doorbell, I get taken by the same sensations as when I'm about to do an EVA: a rush of adrenaline, mixed with calm and utter focus. I hear her footsteps. I comb my hair with my fingers one last time and make sure my shirt is buttoned correctly. The door opens, and there in front of me is Philly. Her hair is shorter, and her face has aged slightly – but she appears almost the same.

'Hi,' she says.

'Hi.'

She leads me to the living room. I recognise some of our furniture. There's the wooden table from her parents, the rug and knitted blankets she'd bought on the cheap. There are the brass candlesticks on the chimneypiece, our cacti and *Ficus elastica*, which have doubled in height. Remains of a previous life, carried with reluctance into a new one – and I feel like one of those remains, too. I wait for Philly to tell me to sit down, but she doesn't. Her arms are crossed, and she gives me the same look of curiosity I know so well – except this time, it's tinted with disdain.

'Thanks for having me over,' I say. 'It's lovely around here.'

'Yes,' she says. 'It's great. Very family oriented.'

'I see.' On the bookshelf, I notice books by authors I've enjoyed reading in the past, whose titles I don't recognise: Ishiguro, Murakami, Rooney. I make a note to look them up later.

'Where are you living?' she asks.

'NovaTech secured a flat for me, near King's Cross. While I sort myself out.'

'It must be quite a shock, coming back.'

'Yes,' I say. 'But I'm slowly getting used to it. It's not too bad. The world hasn't changed as much as I'd expected.'

She nods. We remain standing.

'Here,' I say. 'I brought you some pastries. I got a lemon tart, your favourite. And for Tommy . . . well, I got a selection. I wasn't sure what—'

'You weren't sure what he'd like.'

'Well, no, I wasn't. So, I got a few different ones. Here.'

She takes the box, not paying attention to its contents. 'Thank you.'

'Where is he?' I ask. 'Tommy, I mean—'

'He's in Birmingham. With his grandparents.'

She goes to the kitchen and puts the pastries into the fridge. From the other room, she tells me to sit down. She comes back with a pot of coffee and some biscuits. I ask her about her job, and she tells me she's still at UCL, teaching. That she's been made professor. There's so much more I'd like to know. I'm reminded of my childhood self, who would compose a mental list of questions to ask her and attempt to sprinkle them casually throughout the next day.

'I'm sorry about Shane,' she says, after a pause. 'I always

liked him. And Liv . . . And I know how much he meant to you.'

'Thank you,' I say. And I'm not sure why, for I had been doing well so far in all the times Shane had been brought up, but I feel my emotions swell.

'And your mum too, of course. We were in touch. Until her last day . . .' She grabs a biscuit absentmindedly. 'I'm not sure if it'll make you feel better, but she was very loved, and she knew it. Tommy and her, they were thick as thieves.'

'Thank you,' I say. I feel my voice begin to shake, and before it breaks, I add, 'I'm glad.'

She puts the biscuit down and pours us coffee. We sip in silence for a while. I take in the bitterness of the drink, feeling her gaze on me.

'Do you have anything to say?' she asks.

'I do. But I'm not sure where to begin.'

She laughs. 'Alright,' she says, shuffling into the sofa. 'I'll start, then.' She considers me for a moment. 'Perhaps you can tell me this. Was it worth it?'

'Worth what?' I ask, despite knowing the answer.

'Leaving Tommy. Leaving me.' She gestures around with her hands. 'Your life here. Shane, your mum, all of it. Was it worth it?'

I've imagined this conversation many times, and yet I have no idea what words will come out of my mouth. 'I don't know,' I say, shaking my head. 'I don't know if I'll ever know, Philly. That's not the answer you want to hear, but it's the truth. I'm sorry.' She waits for me to go on, so I continue. 'It would be easy for me to come back here and beg for forgiveness.'

'We were a family,' she says. 'And you broke it.' Her whole body is tense, her arms crossed tightly on her chest. 'And you've never been able to give me one solid reason. One true reason, I mean. Not those bullshit ones about how this is bigger than any of us.'

I want to open up to her – I want her to be able to see all my doubts, my confusions, my constant heartache. 'I think . . .' I begin saying, unsure of myself. 'I believed that if I accomplished many things, many goals that you could consider *unique* – the Navy, the missions, Europa . . . perhaps, it would give my life some sort of greater meaning. That it would give all of the different pieces of my life a deeper, more beautiful cohesion, with a greater purpose. But perhaps . . . perhaps I failed to take into account the pains and the losses that that cohesion would cause.'

Her face stays hardened. She glares at me. '*We* should have been your greater purpose, Ollie.'

My fingers dig into the sofa. 'Maybe . . . maybe that's true.' She scoffs, and I continue. 'But you and Tommy . . . you're doing well, right?'

'We are,' she says, and I catch a glimmer of pride. 'We're doing really well.'

'My dad told me that Tommy reminds him of both of us.' She's smiling now. 'He's got our best traits.'

'That's good,' I say. 'I'm sure you've been the best mum.'

'I've done alright, I think,' she says. 'Considering the circumstances.'

She uncrosses her arms, passes me the biscuits, taking hers again. I'm not yet used to that much sugar, and when I take a bite, I restrain myself from grimacing. Philly observes me as I eat.

'So, is it just you two, then?' I ask, after some hesitation.

'Yes,' she says. 'I was seeing someone for a couple of years, when Tommy was young. But not anymore.'

'Oh,' I say, hiding my disheartenment. 'I'm sorry.'

'I'm surprised no one told you. It was on the news at the time. The tabloids got hold of it. "Astronaut's wife caught with new lover while hero husband is in space" – I believe that was the *Mail*'s headline.'

'Oh, God, that's awful. I had no idea. I'm so sorry—'

'Of course, they didn't know we were separated, back then.' The words feel like a punch. I had known that we were – but neither of us had ever uttered it.

She holds the rest of her biscuit, forgetting it's there. 'You're right, you know. I don't think I'll ever be able to forgive you. But that doesn't mean I don't want you to have a relationship with Tommy. For his sake. And yours, too.' Her voice breaks. 'I don't hate you, Ollie. It's just . . . it'll take time. It's a shock for us too, you know, having you back. And Tommy . . .' She shakes her head. 'He is so kind, and so good. It'll take time. For all of us to work it out . . . for you to become his father again.'

'I know,' I say. I think about coming closer to her, to comfort her, but I stay seated. 'I understand.'

'You were gone a long time, Ollie. His whole childhood.'

'But . . .' I say, 'are you happy?' I think about Liv, asking me the same about Shane, with urgency and love. Philly grabs a napkin from the table, and wipes her eyes with it.

'Yes,' she says, earnestly. 'It's a different kind of happiness from when I was with you. We were so in love, weren't we? We went through so much together. So many ups. But so many downs, too. We were apart almost all the time, by the end. And even when we were together, it felt like we came from different worlds, you and I. Like we couldn't fully understand each other. And it was like we were holding on to something that was already gone – like our marriage was built more on memories than anything else. It felt lonely. And now, well, perhaps the highs are not quite as high. But the lows are not nearly as low. And I've had Tommy, of course . . . So, yes, we're happy. I'm happy.'

'Good,' I say. 'That's what I really wanted to hear. I thought of you two so much.'

'Well, I hope so,' she says, and I see that she's smiling kindly. I feel the tears coming again. I worry that if I stay, I'll say or do something I'll regret. I put my mug down, perhaps too abruptly. 'I should go,' I say. 'I have a meeting with NovaTech soon.' As I'm about to get up from the sofa, I add, 'But maybe . . . we could do something with Tommy soon?'

'Yes,' she says. 'He's coming back from my parents next week. He wants to see you. He might be a bit shy at first but, well, I'm sure you'll find ways to connect.'

We hug each other, stiffly. I see her hesitate, considering the bookshelf. 'Here,' she says. She takes an envelope from it. 'I wrote you a letter when you were away. Of course, I couldn't send it to you. But it helped me, writing it. Here. You can read it once you're home, if you'd like.'

I clutch it and thank her. She walks me to the door. Before leaving I have the urge to turn around one last time, but I do not. Instead, I go down her front steps, my feet heavy on the landing, and I walk towards the station.

30

I have some time to kill before my train, so I wander to the park. I find a bench by the lake, opposite two swans swimming near the waterlilies. In the background, I can hear the melody of the ice-cream van, mixing with the sound of families laughing, of young children on their bikes cycling on top of rustling leaves. In my pocket, Philly's letter presses against my chest.

I'm not sure what I expected. The pain and the surreal nature of the situation, her anger and distance – I knew they would be there. Of course I still loved her. But I no longer felt the romantic love that had once been so inseparable from my being. Perhaps she was right. Perhaps what I held on to up there on *Talos* was nothing but a distant image of us, one that we had long outgrown – like when we gaze at stars, which in truth have long been dead.

I think of Masuda on *Late Night*, saying, *It's just part of the job*. I think of the photograph of his children looking at him through the blinding sun, and of *Pegasus*'s wreckage, a hearse wandering aimlessly in the universe. I think of Professor Whitley, shuffling papers behind his cluttered desk. I reach for Philly's letter. I unfold it carefully, and begin to read.

London, November 2032

Ollie –

I feel stupid, writing to you like this. But I was talking to Liv – we went for a drink on Saturday, near her work. She said that writing letters to Shane like this helped with her grief.

She called it that: grief. Of course, you and Shane are not dead. You're out there, somewhere in the universe, on your big adventure. How are we supposed to grieve someone who's not dead?

It's been four years now, since you left. The first year, I was under the delusional impression that you were going to come back at any moment. That this was nothing but a big practical joke. Or that one of you would realise that, hey, there's been a mistake, that you must abort the mission and make a U-turn. But I don't think like that anymore.

Tommy and I went trick-or-treating last week. Can you guess what he wanted to wear? An astronaut costume. Just like Daddy, he said, and it broke my heart. So, there I was, looking for astronaut costumes for nine-year-olds. They don't teach you this in the parenting books. They don't tell you how to deal with your child wanting to dress like his dad, who abandoned him to go to space.

Sometimes, I wonder if you and I could have spared one another a lot of pain, if we had just stayed friends. If that day in Glasgow, after Shane and Liv had caught their train, I should have said my goodbyes right then and there, and made my way back to Edinburgh before dinner. But then I see Tommy, and the thought vanishes. He is a good kid, Ollie. Handsome like his dad, curious like I was at his age. I have a feeling he might not follow our scientific paths, though. He asked me for some watercolour paints for Christmas, and canvas and brushes. In the new year, once the temperature warms, I'll take him camping somewhere so that he can paint the outdoors. I know there's no point in saying it, but I will: I wish that you could come with us.

Your mum passed away a year ago now. This week, we went to visit her grave. Tommy crouched down, and began talking to her in whispers. I backed away, to give them some space. I read the tombstone. 'Alice Elizabeth Ines', it said. 'Beloved mother, wife and daughter'. I saw daisies beginning to sprout to the side of the grave, and a bee hovering by the flowers we had brought. I saw a peacock butterfly land on top of the tombstone, just above her first name, and a crop of dandelions growing at its feet. I saw an Earth burgeoning with life, your son in its midst, and I imagined you, up there on your own, searching for more of it. I thought of all the things you have missed and will miss, right here on Earth: the planet where you belong, among the people who loved you with all their being. And, for the first time, instead of anger or sadness, I felt sorry for you.

Wishing you well always,
Philly x

PHOENIX MISSION
Commander Oliver Ines's Personal Log

Talos, Day 3650.

We begin the descent. The heat rises into our suits. Dom drifts in and out of consciousness. Lucia is clinging to her seat, her eyes firmly shut, muttering what I think are prayers. I see Earth approaching, from a dot to a globe to all-encompassing. I see its details, its curves come to life, calling to me. I distinguish waves and ripples in the sea. I can almost feel it – my body submerged in ice-cold water.

There is light everywhere, blinding in its brightness. I have not seen the like of it in so long. To the east I see the sun rising, a fiery welcome. Sweat obscures my vision, and I wipe it away with the back of my glove. The whole deck is shaking. Dom and Lucia's bodies toss from side to side, her mutters now shrieks.

I think about what awaits me down there. My father in his garage, my mother perhaps, miraculously recovered, picking ripe fruits from our garden. Tommy, now a teenager – his grey-blue eyes so akin to mine, filled with hatred or love, recognition or disbelief, I'm not sure. I picture Philly the last time I saw her, her worn-out face, her shudder as I touched her.

There will be fame, too, and there will be glory. There will be Shane's death, breaking into the open, like water from a shattered vase.

There is more heat, and there is more light, and again it blinds me. If I could reach my hand a little further, out into the open, I feel certain I'll be able to touch it. To grasp its very core, to merge with it and become one.

And then, beneath the shaking and the engine's sound, beneath Lucia's yells and my shallow breath, I hear a shrill, high-pitched noise, barely discernible, but undoubtedly there – not unlike the sound of the cicadas, which had called to me in my youth.

Acknowledgements

To my agent Matthew Turner: thank you for your unwavering belief in my writing and in me since day one.

To Kishani Widyaratna, my brilliant, patient editor, without whom this book would not be, and to my American editor Retha Powers, thank you – what a privilege it has been to work with you both.

To the whole team at 4th Estate: Aoife Inman, Nicola Webb, Eve Hutchings, Hope Butler, Ellen Woodley, Jay Ramchandar, Molly Lo Re, Julian Humphries, Chris Gurney, Paul Erdpresser, and many more: thank you for all the work and passion you have poured into this book – it really does take a village. Thank you also to Hazel Orme and Martin Bryant, for their sharp and clever eyes, and to the very talented Jack Smyth, for his cover illustration.

My immense gratitude to the whole team at Rogers, Coleridge and White, particularly Peter Straus, Sam Coates, Tristan Kendrick, Stephen Edwards, Katharina Volckmer, Aanya Davé, Sampurna Ganguly, Maddie Luke and Laurence Laluyaux, for being the most fervent champions of my writing, and for finding it so many readers across the world.

My deepest thanks to University College London's Department of Physics and Astronomy, for letting me attend some of their lectures, which provided me with much-needed knowledge in astrophysics and our solar system.

I'm also indebted to Michio Kaku's *The Future of Humanity*, for acquainting me with some of the intricacies and obstacles that space travel faces. And for anyone wanting to learn more about life on the International Space Station and the European space industry (much fictionalised in my novel), I highly recommend Tim Peake's excellent autobiography *Limitless*.

All scientific inaccuracies in the book are of course entirely my own mistakes, or have been rendered so purposefully to serve the fictional elements of the story.

The Familygram information on p. 123 was taken from the Royal Navy website. On p. 215, the expression 'when they remained the still point of my turning world' is paraphrased from a line in the great poem that is 'Burnt Norton' by T. S. Eliot.

Thank you to my early readers, Hope Ndaba, Dredhëza Maloku and Greg Clowes, as well as my dear friend Isabella Childs: how lucky I am to have kind and bright friends like you.

To all the booksellers, journalists, bloggers, writers and readers who have supported my writing in one way or another, thank you: I am forever grateful to you.

To Stephen and to Gillian, lovely Gill, who had many stories, too – thank you for all the kindness you have shown me.

Thank you to my family, my parents and sisters, whom I love very much: let's never let go of each other.

And finally, thank you to Jack. Seven!